# MESSAGE
# in the BONES

Dawn Merriman

**Dedication**
This book is dedicated to my wonderful husband, Kevin, and my children. Thank you for always supporting me. Also dedicated to Lori Ream for pushing me to finish and for all her insights and encouragement.
*-Dawn Merriman*

# Chapter 1

## GABBY

*Freak* is a nasty word. It burns like a slap.

A group of teenagers sit behind me at the coffee shop tucked inside the superstore.

"Isn't that the psychic freak?" one of them asks the others.

My quiet evening of people-watching with a mocha latte ruined, I turn on the teenagers.

"Didn't your parents teach you better manners?" I demand from my seat at the next table.

The two males and a young girl with a nose ring stare in shock that I confronted them. The boys look startled, the young woman has the good grace to look ashamed.

"We're sorry," she says, fidgeting with her hair. "Tell her you're sorry," she says to her companions.

They mumble something that can loosely be described as an apology.

I turn back to my latte, my cheeks flaming in embarrassment.

They whisper together, thinking I can't hear them.

"Ask her," one boy urges the other.

"Leave her alone," the girl scolds.

I know what's coming next. The question everyone asks.

I beat them to the punch.

"I don't know if you will win the lottery," I say loudly.

The girl giggles.

Choosing people-watching from the coffee shop as a fun activity says more about me than it does about River Bend, Indiana, but there isn't too much to do here. We do have an antique covered bridge and an amazing park nestled along a bend of the St. Joe River. I often run at the park, but a rainstorm took the park off my list of options for tonight.

The rain must have driven the kids inside as well. At least they have friends to hang out with.

My latte and a book keep me company.

A very young boy wanders by the half-wall separating the coffee shop from the rest of the store.

I forget the teenagers and focus on the child.

His hair is the improbable shade of blond only the very young are blessed with and women spend hundreds of dollars trying to reproduce. His chubby face looks curiously around him, not scared yet, but working towards it. The closer I get to thirty, the more I enjoy watching children, and this little guy radiates cuteness.

Instinctively, I look for his mother, but he walks alone. He wanders past the half-wall separating the coffee shop from the store then totters towards the produce section and its bright colors.

The delicate cross tattoo on my left inner forearm begins to tingle, telling me to act. Rubbing it through the fabric of my jean jacket doesn't make the tingle stop. I down the last of my coffee and leave the teenagers twittering behind me.

I find the little boy near a display of dried fruit. Scanning the produce section, I still don't see a mother looking for a lost child. The fact annoys me. I kneel close to the little boy. We are alone between the dried fruit display and the organic tomatoes.

"Hi there, are you lost?"

He turns his angelic face to me, cocks his head sideways.

"Don't think so." His tiny voice is as cute as his face.

"Where's your mommy?"

"Around." He points to a package of dried apricots. "Can I have this candy?"

"That's not candy, hunny."

Looking around one more time, I can't find a frantic parent.

I slip the glove off my left hand, the only hand that actually needs one.

I rarely make a contact on purpose, but the insistent tingle of my tattoo forces me to make an exception.

The boy puts his chubby palm on mine. I close my eyes and open my mind.

*Laughing, running, a shaggy dog, the sweet taste of candy, snuggling with Mommy.*

So far nothing helpful, just fuzzy impressions of a

young boy's mind. I focus harder on Mommy.

*Tall, blonde, safe, smells like vanilla.*

"What was Mommy doing when you last saw her?" I ask the boy.

"Talking," he answers simply. I do what I can with that, try to see what he saw.

*Tall, blond, wearing a red jacket. Talking to another woman, not paying attention to the boy. Boxes of cereal behind her.*

"Let's go find Mommy, ok?" I slip the glove back on and take his chubby hand in mine, ignoring the pang of longing stirring inside me.

The blonde mother talks to another woman in the cereal aisle, completely unaware her son had run off.

He pulls away and runs to his mom. "Mommy!"

I recognize the woman and groan inwardly. Lacey Aniston. She's on the evening news now, but I knew her before the nose job. She never needed one. Lacey was the prettiest girl in high school and made sure you knew it.

I approach slowly, although I'd rather run away. Lacey finally notices me and nearly breaks out laughing. "Hey look," she says to her companion. "It's Gabby McAllister." She makes my name sound like a bad word. I know the other woman, too. Ashley and Lacey were tight friends back in school.

I force my feet to walk closer to them.

"I found him in the produce section," I say by way of explanation.

"Really? Bryce, did you wander off again?" Lacey says sweetly to the boy, unconcerned.

10

"Hi, Gabby," Ashley says, politely. "How are you doing?"

I shrug, not trusting her.

Ashley pushes on, "How's your mom?"

"She's doing as well as can be expected," I answer vaguely.

"I've thought about you guys a lot over the years." Ashley glances at Lacey, then leans closer and lowers her voice, "I always wanted to tell you how sorry-."

"Stop any fires lately?" Lacey interrupts with the old joke, laughing openly at me. Ashley looks away uncomfortably.

"Well, now you have your son back." I motion to Bryce and shove my gloved hands deep into my jacket pockets. Lacey doesn't say thank you. I walk away, calling "You're welcome," over my shoulder.

"Nice gloves, Gabby," Lacey calls after me. Her laughter echoes off the cereal boxes as I leave.

I resist the urge to run down the aisle.


Once in the parking lot, I do run, but blame it on the rain. The worst of the thunderstorm has passed, but water pours down the windows of my beat-up Dodge Charger, blocking me from the world.

I scream in frustration.

The fire incident still stings after ten years. In a town where little ever happens, mistakes like that stick with you.

Except it wasn't a mistake. No one remembers that part.

I was sixteen at the time. Mom and Dad had been gone for over a year by then. My older brother, Dustin, and I lived with Grandma Dot, trying our best to pretend our life was okay. Dustin adjusted well to our situation. A star athlete on the basketball team and popular in school, he transitioned with ease.

I struggled. My world shattered at fifteen, a delicate age. I started feeling things I couldn't explain with my left hand. Things I shouldn't know.

I'd feared telling Grandma Dot, but she supported me and understood. She had her own version of my ability and said I got it from her. Our shared secret skill drew us closer.

Dustin hated the whole concept of psychic ability. I tried talking to him about it once and his open disgust taught me to keep quiet.

The night of the basketball game I had no choice.

I sat with Grandma Dot in the stands, feeling self-conscious. The other kids were having fun together, and I only had Grandma to sit with. Dustin captained the team. I enjoyed watching him and supporting him but had trouble getting into the game.

I got restless and went for a walk. Roaming the halls of the school alone, I trailed my left hand along the wall. Killing time until the game ended and we could leave.

My hand slid along the brick wall, then across the metal door of a utility room. The metal of the door felt cool, but the shock of touching it nearly burned my hand. Curious, I put my left palm flat on the door.

The jolt terrified me.

*Fire, smoke, heat, fear, danger, run, run, fire, fire!*

I panicked. I admit that. I over-reacted. I admit that too.

But real fear pounded through me.

"Fire!" I screamed, my voice echoing off the brick walls. A few people outside the gym looked at me curiously. "Fire! Run!" They looked around, no smoke, no flames. One man approached me to help, but I shot past him.

I slammed through the double doors leading to the gym full of people watching the game. Both sets of bleachers full of cheering people, the players passing and shooting the ball, and the cheerleaders jumping through their routines on the sidelines were all in danger.

"Fire!" I screamed in terror. I ran right into the court, instinctively going to Dustin. "Everyone get out, the building's on fire!"

The crowd went silent. The cheerleaders stopped cheering. The players lost track of the ball and it bounced to the other end of the court. Every eye focused on me, except Dustin. He kept his back turned, too ashamed to look. No one ran to safety.

"I said the building's on fire. Everyone has to get out!" I screamed at the bleachers.

A few people stirred and headed for the doors, not willing to take the chance. Once they started out, a few more followed in a slow stream.

The coach stormed across the court at me. "What are you talking about? What fire? The alarms aren't going off. We're in the middle of a game here." Angry spittle

13

flew from his mouth onto my face.

"The utility room's on fire. Why won't anyone believe me?" I looked around in confusion, wanting Dustin. He kept his back to me and hurried to the far end of the court to retrieve the basketball.

A strong, wiry arm wrapped around my waist, Grandma Dot. "Gabriella, what's going on?"

"I touched the utility room door. I saw fire." Grandma Dot stiffened next to me, understanding.

"Show me." She led me off the court.

Laughter rolled through the room. Countless angry mouths and uncaring eyes ignored the danger and laughed at me, the new joke of the town.

Grandma Dot led me away. I looked over my shoulder for my brother. Dustin pretended he didn't know me. His betrayal stung more than the laughter from the crowd.

People pushed past me to return to the game, giving me harsh looks.

"You should be ashamed of yourself," more than a few of them grumbled at me.

"How dare you scare us like that?" one woman accused.

Grandma Dot flashed her eyes at the woman and she scurried away.

A man in a suit strode over with authority, his shoes clipping the floor in anger.

"It's illegal to yell 'fire' in a crowd for no reason," he barked at me. "Not a funny prank, young lady."

"Don't you threaten my granddaughter," Grandma Dot snapped at the man. "If Gabby says there's a fire, then

14

there is a fire."

The man started to say something then shut his mouth.

"Open this door, and let's see," Grandma challenged.

The man hesitated. "I'll get the keys." His shoes clipped away.

Grandma Dot leaned close to my ear. "You better be right or we're in trouble."

"I sensed fire."

Grandma Dot touched the door herself and closed her eyes. Her powers aren't as strong as mine, and she shook her head.

The man came back with the keys and slid one into the metal lock. He looked at me in warning before he opened it. "Last chance to tell the truth."

"Open it," I said.

He turned the key and pulled the heavy metal door.

# Chapter 2

## GABBY

I held my breath as the key turned in the lock, afraid of what we'd find behind the door.

The gray metal panel swung open.

The sickening smell of burning plastic poured over us. Smoke pooled at the ceiling.

The administrator cursed and rushed into the utility room. He grabbed a fire extinguisher off the wall and located the small electrical fire in the back corner.

A short blast of the extinguisher and the fire went out.

He joined us outside the door, coughing and waving at the air.

He stared at me with a mixture of amazement and fear. "How did you know?"

I squeezed Grandma Dot's hand, frightened that I had been right. "I'm glad you put it out. I was scared and no one was listening to me."

His eyes narrowed with suspicion. "Did you start this fire?"

"Of course she didn't," Grandma Dot snapped at the man. "How could she? The door was locked."

The man backed away from me, not wanting to hear how I knew.

The smoke had cleared from the room. He put the extinguisher back and hurried away shaking his head.

"Can we go home now?" I pleaded with Grandma Dot. "There's no way I'm going back to the game and I'm never coming back to school."

"It will blow over," Grandma Dot soothed. "Things always blow over."

But it didn't blow over.

Grandma Dot made me go back to school no matter how hard I begged. High school kids are cruel. Dramatically yelling "Fire!" when they saw me in the hall became a running joke.

The rumor spread that I had psychically sensed the fire. The town ate that up. I had grown used to the sidelong glances and barely hidden comments behind my back when I lost my parents. Crazy, freak and witch were just new words added to the gossips's mouths.

Fake was another popular word.

No one mentioned the fire was real, or that I saved countless lives.

Lacey Aniston enjoyed throwing it in my face tonight. Lacey had been a cheerleader at the basketball game and had a front-row seat to my screaming on the court.

I scream now in my car.

I turn the key, and the Charger rumbles to life.

I stomp on the gas pedal and head out into the country, hoping a drive through the corn fields will take the edge off my anger.

The Charger and I speed down the wet country roads, music blaring from the battered speakers. I yearn to see something new, to go where no one knows me.

The rain stops, and I keep driving.

The roads start to dry, and I keep driving.

Four towns away, I stop for gas and a sandwich. I sit at a small table in the gas station, munching my tasteless ham and cheese. Strangers come and go. No one even glances at me.

I bask in the anonymity.

It's a straight shot down the four-lane highway to home. A much quicker path than the winding way I came. Much more traffic, too.

A red Camaro pulls past me. Feeling ornery, I push the gas, hoping to get the Camaro to race.

The Charger rumbles louder, gains speed. I push the pedal harder, slide past the Camaro. It doesn't take the bait. Letting up on the gas, I slip back in line next to the red car. The middle-aged driver ignores me, unimpressed with my antics. He keeps his attention on the road as a responsible driver should.

I'm not in a responsible mood.

I slam the pedal and dart ahead with a little squeal of the tires. The speed intoxicates me. What's the point in being called crazy if you can't act crazy once in a while?

Flying down the left lane, I pass a small car, a pick-up truck, and a minivan. "Eat my dust!" I yell dramatically and laugh out loud at my childishness. "Whoo-who!"

A sedan rides up on my right. I push the gas even harder, ready to pass it in a flash. Pulling alongside the sedan, I look towards the driver, laughing and enjoying myself.

I don't see his face. The insignia on his car door grabs my attention instead.

Red and blue lights flick on, their intention clear.

"Crap on a cracker!" I yell at the dashboard. Slowing down, I pull over to the gravel shoulder of the highway, fear swimming in my gut.

The cop parks behind me and the officer takes his time reaching my window.

"Please don't be Dustin. Please don't be Dustin." I repeat as I watch the officer approach in my side-view mirror. My brother Dustin is the head detective with the River Bend police department. Unlikely he's out doing traffic stops, but on a small force, everyone pitches in.

The officer knocks on my window. I should have rolled it down already. I know the drill well enough. I push the button and the tinted window slides down, revealing crisp blue eyes and neatly cut hair.

"Thank God, Lucas, it's just you." Dustin doesn't have

to pull over his crazy sister.

"Gabby, what are you doing out here driving so fast?" Lucas Hartley leans his forearms on my open window. "You could kill someone driving like that." My brother's partner normally smiles when he sees me, but not tonight.

"I didn't know you did traffic stops, Officer." I school my face to look innocent and sweet, look up through my lashes, and blink in an exaggerated way.

Lucas sees through my ploy. "Don't try that flirty stuff on me, Gabby. I know you too well to think you're serious." His face softens.

"It was worth a try." The smile on my face surprises me. "Why are you out here doing traffic? No big cases to investigate right now?"

"Olivia wants to take ballet lessons. I'm picking up a few extra shifts to help pay for them."

"How is Olivia? I haven't seen her in a long time."

"Sassy as ever and growing like a weed. She was here this weekend, but is back in Indianapolis with her mom now." I catch the note of longing in his voice. Lucas and Amber had a short, ill-advised marriage. He met her in Indianapolis on his first post as a police officer, but he brought her back to River Bend to raise their daughter Olivia. Amber didn't like the small-town life and soon left Lucas and headed back to the big city, taking Olivia with her. Lucas was well established in the police department by then and decided to stay on. He gets to see Olivia every other weekend.

Silence fills the car, the red and blue lights dance across my dashboard. Lucas looks at my mouth, waiting for me to say something.

A car rushes past us on the highway, bringing us back to the present. Lucas places his hands on the window. "Right, speeding. You didn't tell me why you were driving so fast. Everything okay?"

His interest both touches and annoys me. "Why wouldn't it be?"

He blows out air in exasperation. "Have you been drinking tonight?"

"Why's that always the first question you guys ask?" I try on the sweet innocent face again.

Lucas chuckles, making his tool belt jangle. The sounds mix together nicely. "Answer my questions, Gabby. Have you been drinking? I can give you a breathalyzer if I need to."

"You don't want to do that. You want to let me go home with a warning. I will drive slow and safe the whole way. Just like Grandma Dot on her way to church."

This really makes him laugh, jangling his tools again. "Don't drive like Grandma Dot, or I'll have to haul you into lock up."

"So I can go home then?" I ask sweetly.

He searches my face with his trained cop eyes, looking for signs of impairment. His eyes linger a moment on my lips again. I lick at the sudden dryness.

"I'll give you a warning this time. But no more late-night racing. Or any racing for that matter." He straightens, removing himself from my open window.

"Thank you, Lucas," I say earnestly. "You won't tell Dustin, will you?" I finger the edge of my jacket, waiting for his answer.

"I won't tell Dustin. Your secret's safe with me. Now go home and go to bed." He turns on his heel, raising a hand in a half-wave goodbye. I watch him in the side-view mirror all the way back to his car.

# Chapter 3

## DUSTIN

My arms shake under the weight of the bench press. Two more and I've finished my reps for today. I lay back on the bench, focusing on the open rafters of my basement gym. Gritting my teeth, I push up. A low growl escapes as I lift the weight. I hold the weight above my chest, take a breath, and prepare to lower it again. I upped the weight this morning, another step on my personal workout plan. The first day at a new weight is the hardest, but also the most fulfilling.

I lower the bar, careful to control the descent.

"Dustin, you down there?" My wife's question breaks my concentration. I almost drop the weight but catch it on the stand just in time.

I continue staring at the basement rafters.

"Dustin?" Her voice louder now, more insistent.

Walker starts crying upstairs, the shrill unavoidable cry of a young baby. "Coming."

Alexis stands in front of the sink, near the wide window overlooking our front yard. Bathed by the morning sun, she struggles to contain Walker. He flails his chubby arms, pushes against his mom, and screams his displeasure. A surge of pride and protectiveness wells up at the sight of my family.

"Here, let me have him." I take Walker and settle him against my shoulder. He lets rip another wail, directly into my ear, then settles down.

"Look at the mess he made on my new sweater." Alexis dabs at a spit-up stain on her shirt. "Now I have to change it, you little stinker." Alexis takes Walker's chubby hand and kisses it as she leaves to change.

"How'd your workout go?" she calls over her shoulder.

"Upped the weight this morning." I follow behind her down the hall to our room.

Alexis pulls off the dirtied sweater and tosses it into the laundry basket. She pulls another sweater out of her closet, wearing only a bra and her well-fitting pants. I enjoy the eye-full. Since Walker arrived a few months ago, I rarely get to enjoy her body. I'll take whatever I can get at this point.

"You look good in that outfit," I say putting special meaning into my words.

Alexis turns, steps closer, slowly. "Oh, yeah?" She arches her back suggestively, tosses the sweater over her

26

bare shoulder, teasing in a delightful way. I reach to touch her bare skin, eager for the connection.

Walker lets out a wail from my shoulder. I drop my hand, mood broken.

Alexis snaps back into mom-mode, slips the sweater over her head. "I've got to get going. We have baby class this morning." She takes Walker from me and kisses my cheek. "I made your lunch. It's on the counter."

I grab her hand to keep her from leaving the room. Pulling her close, I kiss her on the lips. She sinks into the kiss. "Finish this later?" I suggest.

"Love to." We both know it probably won't happen, but it's nice to think it might.

I shower my workout sweat away and put on my uniform. My pants button a little easier today. Alexis' diet and my workout plan must be doing the trick. "Can't have the next police chief getting out of shape," she'd said in her well-meaning way. I don't care how my pants fit, but if it makes Alexis happy, then I'm happy.

My tool belt settles on my hips with a satisfying weight. I check my gun in its holster, the weight of the Ruger even more satisfying. My lunch waits on the counter. I don't look inside. I'd rather be disappointed by the raw vegetables and fruit slices later.

The October sky stretches over my neighborhood in a shade of blue improbable for this late in the year. Indiana weather is unpredictable, the changing of the seasons more of a suggestion than a set rule. Yesterday it stormed, today the sun shines. The heat and the blue sky contrast with the orange, red and yellow leaves on the trees. I pause by the door to my cruiser, turn my face to the morning sun.

A chorus of shouts echo around the houses of my neighborhood. Frantic voices shatter the beauty of the morning.

Putting my hand on my holster just in case, I run towards the sounds coming from behind the houses. Our street is the last street of homes they built in this neighborhood. Beyond lies an open field of another property. This past week they started moving dirt and working the field in preparation for another housing development.

I run across the backyard towards the shouts on the other side of the tree line, my mind taking in the details as I go. A bulldozer idles, smoke coming from its stack. No driver in the seat, but the machine idles quietly. Doesn't look like an accident there. Some workers mill around the dozer, but no one's laying on the ground, no major injuries. The workers circle around a low pile of dirt and another man tries to keep them back.

One of the men spots me running towards them and jogs over to meet me. It's a guy I picked up on a disorderly conduct charge a few months ago. Lester something.

"Officer McAllister," he says by way of greeting. It's Detective McAllister now, but I don't correct him.

"What's going on Lester? I heard shouts."

"The dozer found something." Lester is jumpy and sweating.

"What did it find?" I ask pointedly.

"Bones." The way he says the word chills me.

A ripple of excitement tingles down my arms.

*Human bones buried in a field and I'm first on the scene. I can't wait to tell Alexis.*

Approaching the dirt piled up by the bulldozer I put on my best cop voice. "Okay, everyone, back up, give me some room." The workers obey and watch me from a short distance.

A large bone pokes out from where the dozer turned the ground. A few smaller pieces litter the dirt, broken by the dozer. Looks like deer bones. A little wave of disappointment washes over me, triggering guilt. I put on a glove and brush the dirt away from the largest bone. It slides out of the pile, broken. Maybe a femur? I brush some more dirt away and reveal a few more broken pieces.

"Should we call 9-1-1?" Lester asks.

"Give me a moment to figure out what we have. It might be a deer or something."

I shuffle closer to the pile, still crouched low, ignoring the twinge of an old basketball injury in my right knee. I dig deeper and a hand emerges. The excitement tingles again. A rounded piece catches my attention. Moving faster now, I expose some more.

It looks like a skull.

I should leave it, should call in the forensic team. Instead, I tug it as gently as possible.

The skull pops loose and rolls down the dirt and bumps into my foot. Startled, I land on my rear.

The skull rolls against my outstretched leg, the sun glinting off the forehead. It smiles up at me with its unmistakable grin.

It doesn't take long for my team to arrive. My team, I like the sound of that.

My partner, Lucas Hartley, arrives first. He hands me a large take-out coffee cup. "Thought you might need one of these this morning."

Expecting plain bitter black, the sweet, creamy latte surprises me. Lucas knows Alexis has me on a diet. My favorite fancy coffees are off-limits, especially with the extra pumps of caramel. I raise my eyebrows in question.

Lucas shrugs conspiratorially.

I sip the latte gratefully and ask, "Did Pete find anything in missing persons?"

"Nothing matches. He's going to check with Fort Wayne too, but it's a long shot. These bones have been here a long time."

"Takes several years to be just bones. That's a wide search."

We crouch next to the bones and the gravity of the case crashes in. I get the strange sensation we're two kids simply playing detectives, not the actual detectives in charge. The initial excitement of the find has worn off, replaced with the impotent fury familiar to law enforcement. This person deserved better than a bullet in the head and a dirt grave in a field. The burden of finding justice weighs heavy.

I resist the urge to dig further into the dirt pile. The femur, the hand, and the skull clearly visible now, Lucas inspects the scene.

"We have nothing to go on," he says quietly. I'm glad he said it so I didn't have to.

"Forensics will find something."

"Hopefully." His voice lacks conviction. After a moment, he continues. "You know she could tell us something now," he says carefully.

"No way. I'm not dragging my sister into this."

"But she could help us," he says evenly. Lucas knows my feelings about Gabby and her "gift." Gabby and I keep our distance. I have fought long and hard to earn my position as detective and respected policeman, despite being dragged down by the town crazy.

"I don't want her near me, or this case." The words come out harsher than I intended.

"So what's your plan then? Hope something falls out of the sky to get the investigation started? We don't know how long this body's been here, let alone who it is. We don't even know how this person died."

I want to do what's best for the investigation, but using Gabby?

Lucas senses my hesitation, "I can call her if you want. She likes me."

"She doesn't like me," I say simply.

"Think how proud Alexis will be when you solve this case, knowing you used everything available to help." He's pushing it now and knows it. But it works, damn him. I have to deal with Gabby, so what? I think of Alexis and Walker and what's best for them, and pull out my cell phone.

"Sometimes I hate you," I grumble to my partner.

Lucas smacks me on the arm, "You're a good man, McAllister."

The call goes to voicemail. I stab at the screen, impatient to hang up.

"She didn't even answer." I shove the phone back in its case on my belt.

"Call her again in a moment, she will." Hartley looks pleased with himself, I want to punch him. I stare down at the skull and focus on the job before us. A few minutes later, I call Gabby again.

# Chapter 4

## GABBY

The beat of the music pounds in my earbuds, matching the beat of my feet pounding on the jogging trail along the river. The early sun sparkles on the river to my right, a blanket of rippling gems. The morning is perfect, marred only by the chafing on my heel from my new running shoes. I push on, enjoying the music, the air, the sun. I lose myself in my run, alone with the trail and my willpower pushing me farther.

An incoming call intrudes through my earbuds. I slow my pace and check the screen.

Dustin.

My wonderful mood pops like a balloon. I resent the power Dustin has over how I feel. Hitting ignore call, I push on with my run. My feet hit the trail with added emphasis. I drive myself faster and welcome the pain of burning legs and tearing breath.

A little while later, I turn away from the river trail and towards the park where my Charger waits. I need to get to work soon anyway.

The phone rings again as I slow to a cool-down jog. Lucas must have told him about pulling me over last night and big brother wants to chastise me. The sting of betrayal surprises. I thought Lucas liked me enough to not tattle to my brother.

Pulling out the earbuds, I punch answer.

"What do you want, Dustin? I'm not in the mood for a lecture," I grumble.

"Hey, Gabby." I barely recognize his uncertain voice.

Panic slides over me.

"Is Grandma Dot okay?" The only reason for him to call and not bark at me.

"What? Of course she is."

"Oh." A wave of relief. "Then what do you want?"

"I need your help." A sharp bark of laughter escapes my lips before I can snatch it back. Dustin never asks for my help.

"Sure you do. Are you and Lucas up to some game? I really don't have time for this." I've reached the Charger in the parking lot now, and lean against the hood while I talk. I catch myself absently rubbing the tattoo on my left forearm. I freeze and stare at my arm. So involved with talking to Dustin, I hadn't felt it tingling.

My voice and manner are serious now. "Dustin, what's going on?"

"Can you come over to that new neighborhood they're putting in behind my house?"

"I'm supposed to be at work soon. Why?"

Silence stretches across the phone line.

"We found some bones, old ones. Obviously a murder victim. We have no idea who it is or where to start. Can you come and, uh, you know?"

Even when asking for my help, he can't say the words out loud.

"Have a vision, you mean. Get a reading. Use my psychic powers." I provide him with some terms he'll never use. My gift is Dustin's biggest shame.

"You know what I mean. Lucas thought maybe you could help." My tattoo burns like bees under the skin now. Telling Dustin no is easy, but I've learned to trust the tattoo. That message comes from somewhere larger than Dustin and I's petty grievances.

"I'll be right there."


The new neighborhood is nothing more than turned dirt and construction vehicles at this early stage of development. Police cruisers and other official vehicles crowd near the back of the site. The yellow crime tape easily points out where the bones wait for me. A shiver shakes my shoulders as I park near the cruisers. I've never done anything like this before. I avoid reading things, even wear gloves to insulate me from touching.

Touching bones on purpose terrifies me.

Fear pins me in the safety of my car. Backing up and

driving away feels like a wonderful idea. My hand reaches for the shifter, wanting to leave. I snap my hand back. I have to do this, no matter how frightened I am.

Pretending more confidence than I feel, I approach the crime scene. Lucas spots me first and hurries over to let me under the tape. Dustin barely looks my way. Fine with me, I'm not here for him anyway.

"Gabby, thank you for coming. I'm sure this can't be easy." Lucas always knows what to say. He holds the tape up for me to duck under. It flutters in the breeze making a sad sound. I hesitate and meet his eyes, questioning.

"You'll be fine. You got this." The genuine smile and kind words give me strength and I step underneath. The yellow tape drops back in place behind me with a snap.

"Not sure what I can do, but I'll try to help."

Lucas leads me to the dirt pile where the bones wait for me. My tattoo burns under my zip-up running sweater. I fight the urge to rub the burning.

Rubbing won't stop it anyway.

"The media's here," Dustin comments by way of greeting and points to a news vehicle pulling in.

"Crap on a cracker," I sigh.

I move slowly closer to the bones gleaming white in the dirt. My whole body tingles now, not just my tattoo.

"Can I get some privacy? Have these other people move back." The small crowd at the scene eyes me with interest, but tries not to show it. Dustin may not have shared his plans with them, but everyone knows who I am and what I do. They're excited for a show.

"Everyone," Dustin's commanding voice draws the

crowd's attention. "Please step over there and give her some space." He doesn't use my name, but I don't care.

The buzz from the bones fills me, much stronger than anything I've felt before. The urge to run nearly wins, but Lucas takes hold of my arm. He leads me to the bones, my feet dragging slow.

The three of us crouch by the dirt pile. Lucas next to me, Dustin nearby. I say a short prayer to center myself. "Lord, let me see what I need to see."

I pull off my left glove and kneel in the dirt. Clods and stones poke my knees.

I ignore the skull smiling at me and reach for the hand bones.

I sense her before I touch her.

A blast of information, stronger than I expected, makes me jerk my hand back.

"It's a woman. Her name is Karen." The crowd behind me twitters and whispers.

"Step back," Dustin barks at them.

I put my hand in my lap, fear slamming through me. Whatever I'm about to see won't be pretty. I can still tell them no, get back in my car and go to work.

Lucas leans close and whispers, "It's okay. You can do this."

I don't share his confidence, but I trust God and my tattoo. I squeeze my eyes shut and ask God for strength to do what he needs me to.

I close my bare hand on her boney one.

*Love, excitement, anticipation, freedom. She's packing, planning. Knocking on the door, intrusion. Familiar face, annoyance. Fear for her children, nothing else matters but her boys. Her plans will have to wait. Driving in the dark, hurry, get to them. Don't stop, just hurry. Confusion, soft white against her face. Betrayal, fear, disbelief. Stop! Sharp pain sliding in. Hot blood, another sharp stab. Struggling against the hands, against the darkness. Darkness wins.*

The sensations surge through me, terrifying.

I squeeze the hand bones in reaction, crush them in my palm. They disintegrate and fall away as the vision fades.

Exhausted, I slump against Lucas.

Sobs tear through me, tears the woman never had the chance to shed. The fear, the anger, and the pain are mine now.

I shake with the effort to contain them. The vision swamps me and I struggle to remain in the present, remain conscious. Lucas puts his arm around my shoulders and holds me against his vest.

"Gabby?" Dustin's concern snaps me back to the present. "Gabby, are you okay?"

I can't find my voice, just nod my head against Lucas.

Whispers from the crowd drag me to my senses. Lucas still has his arm around my shoulders. I sit up suddenly and push away from him.

Both men search my face, waiting for what I have to say. I struggle to put the impressions into words.

"Her name is Karen. She's a mom, has two boys. She was getting ready to go somewhere. Someone showed up, someone she knew. I don't know who it was, just that she trusted them. She was afraid for her boys and got in a car

38

with the person. She was stabbed. She was so scared." My voice threatens to break.

The men stare at me with a mixture of shock and fear and curiosity.

"You saw all that?" Lucas asks quietly.

"I feel like there's more, but I don't know for sure."

"Any idea when or where?" Dustin is all business.

"Nothing concrete, at least several years ago. She was planning to go somewhere, was excited about a new life, with a new love. Her first impressions were of hope, excitement. Then it ended."

"Anything else?" Dustin pushes.

"They took her in a car, the drive was short. I imagine she lived somewhere close by, but I can't be sure."

"The killer, man, woman, anything?" Dustin keeps pushing.

"I told you I didn't see them clearly. I have no idea. She knew and trusted them, that's it." I'm worn out from the vision and sick of Dustin's questions. "I told you everything. It's not an exact science you know."

"You've been a huge help. Thank you. That couldn't have been easy," Lucas breaks in, soothing the situation.

We all climb from the dirt. I turn my back to the bones, look out across the open field that will soon be full of houses. My fists clench at my side, what feels like a stone in the palm of my left. It's a piece of bone from her hand. The rest of them fell to the ground when I squeezed them, this piece I still have. Not sure what to do with it, I slide my hand into my sweater jacket pocket and drop it there. Zip the pocket closed.

I focus across the field, away from the people watching me. Inside, I'm shattered and tangled. The remnants of Karen's fear pound through my blood. The breeze cools the tears on my cheeks, the sun warms my hair.

I square my shoulders against the emotions and lift my chin.

Back in control of myself, I turn to the questioning faces of the crowd, my brother and my friend. Everyone stares at me, some with fear, some with disgust, some with sympathy. I focus on the sympathetic faces and ignore the rest.

Dustin's face is unreadable.

"I did what you needed. Can I go now?" I ask my brother, pulling my glove back on in a practiced movement.

"Of course." Some remnant of brotherly affection must have bubbled up because he walks me to my car. I try not to read too much into the act. He holds the crime tape up for me, and I duck under, force my feet to walk instead of sprint to my car.

Out of the corner of my eye, I see a news camera pouncing. Lacey Aniston follows close behind the camera, microphone in hand. I don't have the energy to face her right now. Talking to the woman twice in as many days is just too much.

"Detective McAllister, is it true you found the bones of a murder victim here this morning?" Lacey starts in with her questioning.

"No comment." Dustin blocks me from the camera and Lacey.

"Did this woman perform a psychic reading on the bones?" Lacey continues her questions.

"This is an ongoing investigation. No comment."

"Did you see anything when you touched them?" She directs her question to me, giving up on Dustin and his standard answer. "Get a close-up of her," Lacey says to the cameraman.

The cameraman obeys and shoves the camera too close. I duck away. Dustin steps towards the camera, forcing the man to back up enough so I can open my car door.

"Gabby, what did you see? Do you know who the killer is?" Lacey's voice is high and insistent, hoping for anything from me before I can get away.

"Leave me alone, Lacey. I have nothing to say." I climb into the car and slam the door. The camera practically pushes against the car window trying to get a shot of me. Thankfully, the tinted windows block most of his view.

"This woman has nothing to do with our investigation. As I said, no comment," Dustin says in his best police voice.

*This woman?* The impersonal way he mentioned me stings. But what did I expect him to say? "This is my sister, Gabby McAllister. She's a crazy psychic, but we need her." Yeah, right.

My emotions tumble and tears threaten. I need to escape.

I turn the key and the rumble of the old engine startles the camera away. I hit the gas harder than necessary and pull away before the camera can catch me crying.

Or worse, Dustin sees my tears.

# Chapter 5

## GABBY

My hands shake on the wheel and sobs choke me. I gasp for air and speed away from the crime scene.

The alarm on my phone startles me and I swerve as I struggle to punch the off button. I need to head to work now or I'll be late.

I'm shaking so badly, it takes three tries to dial the number to the catalog call-center. I tell my boss I'm too sick to work today and hang up before he can ask any questions. I told him the truth. I am sick.

Waves of nausea roll through me, clenching in my gut.

I pull to the side of the road, jump out of the car and hurry to the ditch. Vomit splatters the dried weeds, running down the stalks in disgusting brown rivulets.

I drop to my knees on the side of the road. The dusty gravel and hot tar mix with the vomit stench. Another wave clamps my stomach.

The fresh vomit splashes on the first pile in a grotesque squishing sound. I huddle on the side of the road, my arms wrapped tight around my waist. I squeeze my eyes shut against the replay of Karen's murder. Eyes open or closed, the terror she felt in the last moment fills me.

Birds sing in the nearby trees. The brown leaves rattle like bones. A shudder runs across my shoulders. I wrap my arms tighter against my waist and rock like a child.

A car slows down, intruding. I will it to keep driving. It passes by, leaving me alone in my misery.

The nausea passed, I struggle to my feet.

I ache with emptiness.

The child in me longs for home.


Several cars fill the gravel lot in front of Grandma Dot's beauty shop that she runs from her two-story farmhouse. I park in the family area and let myself into the kitchen.

The familiar scents of herbal tea and Grandma Dot's baking mix with the chemicals seeping in from the beauty shop. I take a deep breath of my childhood and it welcomes me like a comfortable blanket.

I rinse out the taste of vomit and wash off the tears at the kitchen sink. Grandma Dot's voice floats through the sliding doors separating the beauty shop from the rest of the house. The other ladies laugh in reply. For over 40 years, Grandma Dot has done hair for nearly everyone in

River Bend. They come for her entertaining stories as much as for her talent with a comb and scissors.

I slide the door open and slip into the beauty shop. The bright lights and mirrors make me blink.

Jet, Grandma's tiny black mop of a dog, runs to meet me, dancing and spinning for my attention. I gladly scoop him in my arms and hide my face in his fur.

The usual morning ladies sit around the shop, either waiting for their weekly wash and set, or just enjoying the gossip. I receive the usual mixed bag of greetings from the ladies, a few warm smiles and a few averted glances. Everyone here knows me, but not all of them feel comfortable around me. The ones with the most to hide are the most afraid. As if I can sense their secrets just by looking at them.

"Gabriella, what a surprise," Grandma Dot exclaims, pausing in her teasing and back-combing to give me a quick hug. Her tiny, powerful frame feels wonderful in my arms. I cling longer than necessary.

Grandma notices my clinginess and raises her eyebrows at me.

"Dustin found a body this morning," I blurt out. "Well bones, actually."

The ladies gasp. The ones who wouldn't look at me before focus on me now. One woman in the waiting area stares at me, meeting my eyes in the large mirrors covering the far wall of the beauty shop.

"Where?" she asks. The woman looks familiar, but I can't think of her name.

"That field where they're putting in the new housing

addition. The one behind Dustin's house." All eyes are on me, I almost enjoy the attention.

Questions fire at me now. "Who is it? What happened? Were they murdered?" I don't know who to answer first or if I'm allowed to talk about it at all.

"She's a woman and she was murdered," I say bluntly. "I don't know if I should say anything else."

Another round of gasps.

Grandma Dot hasn't said anything yet. She watches me intently, the combs in her hands suspended above Mrs. Mott's pouf of pale purple hair.

"How do you know?" Mrs. Mott asks in her gentle way. "Were you there?" Mrs. Mott has been a weekly customer and close friend of Grandma Dot's for years. She has watched me grow since a chubby toddler. She's one of the few people I trust. She believed me about the basketball game fire and even told me my gift was a blessing. "Did you 'see' something?" she asks me now.

Everyone wonders the same thing, but only Mrs. Mott would actually ask me. I care for the woman, but I'm not comfortable discussing my part in this morning's events.

"I don't...."

"Do you know who it is?" the young woman from the waiting area interrupts, saving me from answering.

I hedge around the direct questions. "I'm sorry. I don't think I should talk about it."

"You brought it up, and now you can't talk about it?" another woman snaps.

"I'm sorry. It will be on the news tonight," I offer, suddenly overwhelmed by all the attention. I shouldn't

46

have said anything in front of all these people. I need to escape. "Do you mind if I go upstairs for a while?" I ask Grandma Dot.

"Of course, hunny." The combs in her hands are back to work again. "Take Jet if you want."

The twittering of the ladies fades as I slide the divider door shut behind me.

The boards of the narrow stairway squeak in their familiar pattern as I make my way upstairs to my old room. The yellow daisy wallpaper smiles at me, the matching yellow comforter on the bed welcomes me. Grandma Dot decorated this room in cheery yellow especially for me, an attempt to brighten the darkness that brought us to live here. The happy color works now.

I slip off my running shoes, this morning's exercise feeling like days ago. Tossing my sweater jacket on the floor next to my shoes, I crawl into my childhood bed. I pull the comforter up to my ears, turn on my side and squeeze my eyes shut. Jet lets me hold him tight to my chest, a welcome ball of warmth. The sounds of the old farmhouse creak around me, a lullaby I've heard countless times.

It sings me to sleep.


Grandma Dot shakes me awake gently, but I jump in fear anyway. It takes a few moments to remember why I'm in my old room. The shadows lean at different angles now, but I have no sense of what time it is or even what day.

"How long have I been asleep?" I snuggle deeper into

the pillows, wishing to stay forever. Jet snuggles out of our cocoon and climbs on Grandma's lap. "Traitor," I grumble to the dog.

"Just a couple hours. I didn't want to bother you, but Dustin has been calling." Grandma Dot smoothes my hair back from my forehead, brushes her finger over the scar on my eyebrow. Instinctively, I shake her hand away.

"He called you?" I sit up and look for my phone, but can't find it, must have left it in the car.

"He couldn't reach you and figured you might be here." Grandma Dot doesn't need an explanation for why I'm here sleeping in my old room.

"Did he tell you what happened this morning?"

"Only that you did a reading on the bones they found. He needs to get an official statement from you. He didn't go into details." She stands, giving me room to climb out of bed.

Nothing I can tell him is "official".

"How about some tea first and you can tell me the details. I closed the beauty shop, so we can talk. Dustin will be here in a bit."

I make a sound of disgust she has heard me make a thousand times.

She looks over her shoulder with a twinkle in her eye. "He'll probably have that cute partner of his with him."

I pointedly ignore that comment. Grandma Dot is a serial matchmaker. Several couples in town owe their happy marriages to her matchmaking skills. She has tried with me, but so far has failed. Finding my mate is a challenge even Grandma Dot can't overcome.

The smell of herbal tea floats up the stairs, drawing me to the kitchen. Grandma grows her own herbs. She knows what each one does and how to combine them for the best results. I don't recognize this particular mix, but I take the cup anyway and join her at the table. Grandma Dot and I have spent countless afternoons just like this, sitting at the beat-up wooden kitchen table, cups of tea warming our hands, talking about my problems.

It takes three sips of the bitter brew mixed with several spoons of sugar until I can talk about it. Grandma Dot waits patiently, knows direct questions are not the way to get me to open up.

"It was an awfully large thing Dustin asked you to do," Grandma Dot finally says. Apparently, Dustin filled her in on the basic details of the morning. "Especially since he's always dismissed your gift as foolishness." Dustin's treatment of me always gets Grandma's hackles up. Grandma has a little of the gift, too, and takes his dismissal of it personally.

"He must have been desperate." I take another sip of tea, disgusted with myself for making excuses for him. He's never done anything to deserve my loyalty, but I can't help myself.

"I'm proud of you for doing it. It must have been hard."

"That's an understatement. You know I avoid seeing things if at all possible." I hold up my hands, my ever-present gloves covering them. "I knew this would be stronger than anything I've ever seen."

"But you did it. That's the important part. You faced

49

the fear and did it." Her praise sits uncomfortably on me. Her thin hand lands on the back of my gloved one. The slight weight gives me strength.

"Her presence was so strong. I felt her before I even touched her." I stare out the window across the backyard. "Her name is Karen. It buzzed to me before I even took off my glove."

"Karen Jennings?"

"I don't know." I shake my head, not sure if I want the memory to return. "She was going somewhere with a man. Then someone else showed up and it all went wrong. She was so scared." I give her the short version of what I saw. A shiver jerks through me remembering her fear. "I felt her die." I can barely speak the words. That moment will be with me forever, the sharp fear, primal and complete.

"No one should have to live through that."

"No one usually does." I make the words light and teasing, but she reads through it.

"True, they usually take that feeling to the grave." We both stare out the window at the back parking area. "I wish he hadn't asked you to help."

"I think he wishes that, too. I kind of collapsed against Lucas for a moment after and Dustin did ask if I was okay. So that's something." I feel pitiful that his small kindness, so normal for a brother, meant something to me. "Of course, he blew it later. Lacey Aniston hounded me with her camera when I went to leave, and Dustin couldn't even say my name. He called me 'this woman'."

"Oh, Gabriella, I'm so sorry. He'll come around

50

someday." She's said these words to me in this exact spot at the kitchen table so many times before. I no longer believe them, and fool myself I no longer care.

Jet jumps off Grandma's lap and starts to bark. Dustin's cruiser pulls in and parks next to my Charger and the old flat bed pickup of Grandma's, an eclectic collection of vehicles.

"The troops have arrived. I need some more tea to get through this."

# Chapter 6

## GABBY

Dustin and Lucas pour through the back door and into the kitchen. Jet barks, sharp and insistent. The constant yapping jangles my nerves.

Dressed in uniform, the two men seem larger, more imposing. Maybe it's the guns on their hips, or the thick vests they wear under their shirts. The warm, inviting kitchen feels tainted with police in it. The world they represent, a world of crime and pain and fear, contrasts starkly to the safety of the kitchen. I have to remind myself they are simply two men I know.

Jet keeps barking at them until Grandma finally gets him to be quiet. Dustin and Lucas hang near the doorway, seeming uncomfortable. This has never truly felt like home to Dustin the way it has to me. He was sixteen when we came to live here and left soon after graduation. To him, home was our life before. This was just a place to live until he was old enough to leave. He resented everything that brought us here.

"Grandma Dot, so nice to see you," Lucas says and steps into the kitchen, breaking the awkward moment of silence.

"Officer Hartley, always nice to put eyes on such a handsome man," Grandma Dot croons. "Or should I say *Detective* Hartley? Congratulations on your promotion. Both of you."

She looks at Dustin, including him in the praise. He just nods and stands in the doorway.

Ever the gracious and loving host, Grandma Dot climbs out of her chair and goes to Dustin with a big smile and a hug. I fight down anger. She had to go to *him*. Why can't he just act normal? Of course, that's the same thing he always asks me. Maybe neither of us knows what normal is anymore. At least he hugs her back. I might have taken a swing at him if he hurt her feelings.

"Come sit down. Gabriella and I were just having some tea. A nice soothing blend I mixed up special. You all probably could use some today."

"Thanks, Grandma." Dustin finally moves and talks, shifts into police mode. Lucas joins us at the table, but Dustin hovers near the counter, his notebook out.

"So, Gabby. We need you to go over what you saw this morning," Dustin starts.

"I already told you."

"Can you please tell us again?" He uses the word please, but his tone doesn't match it.

I pull Jet into my lap, pulling strength from his tiny body. "Someone came to her house and told her the boys were in trouble. Then they drove somewhere. She was stabbed." I leave out the part about the fear and terror and feeling her die. Those are things I can only share with Grandma.

"Nothing else you'd like to add?"

"What else could there be? I only get impressions. It's not like she talks to me and says 'here's what happened and who did it'." My hands shake and I take a sip of tea to calm them.

"We need to be thorough," Lucas calms. "Is there anything else you can think of that might help? Even if it's small."

"Grandma, you said a name earlier. What was it?"

"I asked if her name was Karen Jennings."

Dustin latches onto the detail. Thankful to have the focus off of me, I slump back in my chair and rub Jet.

"Why did you ask if it was Karen Jennings?"

"The field where you found her belonged to Patrick Jennings until recently. Years ago, Patrick's wife, Karen, ran off with a man she had been seeing on the side. No one ever heard from her again. Everyone assumed she and Steven took off for Vegas or something, started a new life. A bit of a coincidence to find someone named Karen on the Jennings's property."

"When was this?" Dustin's pen waits to write the answer in his book.

"Oh, I don't know. About 20 years ago, I'd say."

"How do you know all this?" Lucas asks.

"Patrick and his boys get their hair cut here. Karen got her hair done too, back then. You know everything that happens in this town eventually gets discussed here." Grandma Dot gives me a conspiratorial smile. She never spills the secrets clients tell her. Code of the hair dresser, she calls it. For some reason, people tell her things they wouldn't tell their closest friends. She's got dirt on everyone, but she doesn't spread it.

"That's what I saw, her anticipating going away somewhere, with someone she loved." I sit up excited for some actual information. "Who's this Steven guy she was supposed to go with?"

"Steven Rawlings. He was married to Diane Rawlings. You know, from the Post Office. Steven and Karen thought no one knew about their relationship, but of course there was talk. Then they took off together and that confirmed it."

"Except Karen never left," I say. The words sit heavy between the four of us. "So where is Steven?"

"Maybe he killed her and took off on his own?" Lucas offers.

"Yeah, maybe," I say. "She was killed by someone she knew. Except, she was excited to be leaving and annoyed when someone knocked on the door. If it was Steven at the door, she would have been happy to see him."

"As you said, what you see isn't exact. It could have been Steven," Dustin says.

"She did get into the car with the person, but what

about the fear for her boys? She thought something was wrong with them, only wanted to get to them. If Steven came to the door, he wouldn't have had to trick her. She was already leaving with him."

"Unless she felt guilty at the last minute. Didn't want to leave her kids," Lucas pipes in. I can tell he's thinking about his daughter, Olivia, who he rarely sees.

The four of us mull this idea over, trying to make sense of it. The moment feels almost homey and comfortable, like a family.

Until Dustin opens his mouth. "This is pointless. We need real information. Not psychic impressions and twenty year old gossip." He's right, but his words sting.

"Then go out and do some actual detective work," I snap at him. "Instead of bothering with your crazy sister and your gossiping grandma."

"That's not what I meant."

"I know what you meant. I always know." I toss Jet off my lap and stand up, nearly knocking my chair over in my anger.

From across the kitchen, Dustin takes an involuntary step away from me.

That step, that tiny movement away from me. Something deep inside me shifts.

I lock eyes with my brother's, the first time we've made eye contact in years. In his eyes, I see clearly what I've always suspected.

Fear.

I stalk across the room, holding his eyes, daring him to look away. Everyone watches silently, even Jet. I step closer to Dustin. His body tenses as I approach. I slide off my left glove, slowly, deliberately. I watch his eyes, desperate to see something to prove I'm wrong.

He looks at me in horror. I'm not a sister. I am a monster.

I reach to touch with my bare hand, praying he won't do what I know he will.

He jerks away in fear before I can touch him.

He's six inches taller than me and solid muscle. A trained cop with a safety vest and gun, but he's afraid of his little sister.

The betrayal burns a scar into my heart.

"At least now I know how you really feel about me," I hiss. "Don't ever ask for my help again."

Slipping my glove back on, I turn my back on my brother.

"Grandma Dot, thank you for everything." I kiss her on the cheek, look at Dustin pointedly as if to say, "See, she isn't afraid of me."

No one knows what to say, just watch me put on my jacket and walk to the door.

Lucas finds his voice first. "Gabby, thanks for your help."

"Anything for *you,* Lucas," I toss over my shoulder and slam the door behind me.


My house looks exactly the same as when I left for my run this morning. So much has happened since then, the fact that my house hasn't changed unsettles me.

I will never be the same.

I sit in my driveway and watch the leaves on the massive trees in my yard flutter in the October breeze. Their colors are bright and wonderful, a stark contrast to my mood. The confrontation with Dustin has left me empty and bruised.

The tingle of someone watching me makes me turn my head. My neighbor, Preston watches me from his driveway. I wave at him. He waves back with a friendly smile. Preston moved in a few months ago. He and I are wave-and-smile neighbors, and only shared a few short conversations. He either doesn't know about my history or doesn't care.

I climb out of the car, surprised when he walks across the yard to me.

"Hey, Gabby, everything okay? You've been sitting out here for a while." Dapples of sunlight filter through the leaves overhead and dance across his dark hair. Preston's only a few years older than me and recently divorced. He has soft eyes and a strong jaw. This small act of kindness from a man I barely know soothes the raw edges left by my brother.

"Aren't you sweet? I just have a lot on my mind today." I manage a strained smile and a little charm.

"I'll bet." He looks at the ground, suddenly uncomfortable and unsure. "I saw you on the afternoon news." He says it in a rush, embarrassed.

My smile disappears in a snap.

"So you thought you'd come talk to the freak directly? Get a story to tell all your friends?" I slam the car door.

His friendly smile turns to hurt. I regret my word instantly.

"What I thought was you would be upset and need a friend." His words are clipped with anger. "Bad idea, I guess."

"Preston, I'm so sorry." I backpedal as hard as I can. "I..., it's just...." I can't find the words. "I'm sorry, it's just been a really hard day. Thank you for being nice, I'm not used to it."

Preston studies me, then takes pity. "Not everyone hates you the way you think they do, Gabby. I think what you do is cool."

This floors me.

"Really?" The tension I caused fades away, his shoulders visibly relax.

"Of course. You're helping in a murder investigation. How cool is that?" His open manner is infectious. I'm suddenly conscious of my running clothes and bed head from my nap.

"I guess it is kind of cool." I try to smooth my hair, but the curls are a lost cause.

Neither of us knows what to say next, the only sound from the leaves overhead.

"Well, anyway," Preston stumbles on. "I just wanted to make sure you're okay."

"Thanks again." I desperately search for something to say, but come up empty. "I should probably go in now."

We wave awkwardly and I hurry into the house.

I lean against the closed door. "What the hell was that? 'I should probably go in now'? Crap on a cracker, no wonder you're still single." I chastise myself.

I'm not too upset. Even after everything that happened today, my breath comes light and happy.

Gentle pressure pushes against my ankle. Chester, my gray and white cat looks up at me. "Hey, buddy, I'm happy to see you too."

# Chapter 7

## DUSTIN

The sun sets in splashes of blood red on deepening navy, tangled colors that match my tangled mood. My shoulders bunch in painful knots, the tightness pulls on my neck muscles, a headache throbs dully. The light from my kitchen window pours out on the landscaping. Fall leaves have gathered under the bushes. I make a mental note to rake them out when I have time. Who knows when that may be now, with this murder case hanging over me.

Alexis appears in the window, holding Walker on her shoulder as she fills a glass of water at the sink. The ache in my shoulders and neck relax a little as I watch my family. Shoving the door of my cruiser open with more force than necessary, I take the front steps two at a time.

My wife's smile of greeting draws me to them. Without a word, I wrap them both in my arms, sink into them. This day has been hell, but I am home.

Allowing myself these few moments of peace, I breathe in the scent of her coconut shampoo mixed with the unique smell of baby. The tightness in my shoulders fades even more. Alexis senses my need and holds me closer. The close crush annoys Walker and he squalls.

We both laugh in a release of nervous tension.

"Rough day?" She pulls away just enough to move Walker to her other shoulder. He quiets down and looks at me with brown eyes, so like his mother's.

"You have no idea." Actually she does. I called her earlier and gave her the rough outline of what was going on.

"Go get a shower and I'll heat up your dinner." I kiss her on the forehead and thank god for the thousandth time for this woman and child.

Showered and changed into flannel pants and a t-shirt, I eat dinner on the couch, my feet up on the recliner part. Steve Harvey asks families absurd questions on Family Feud. The nonsense soothes.

"I had the DVR tape the news for you." Alexis sits down next to me, settles Walker against her to nurse him his dinner.

"Do I want to see it?" I reach for the remote.

"It's mostly about Gabby. But you should watch it."

"Breaking news from River Bend this morning," Lacey Aniston starts out, microphone in hand. The smart suit she wears clings to her in a pleasing way. Lacey and I dated briefly in high school and I have touched the curve of those hips. They do nothing for me now.

"Human remains were found today on the site of the new housing development going in north of town. The police must not have much to go on, as they have called in local psychic Gabriella McAllister."

The camera focuses on Gabby, Lucas and I by the bones. The timing is perfect, Gabby reaches for the bones as Lacey says breathlessly, "What will the psychic see?"

Gabby jerks, then slumps against Lucas. It happens so quickly on tape, it seemed much longer in person. "Judging by her reaction, she must think she's had a vision," Lacey says, then keeps talking. I can't listen to her, I am focused on Gabby.

Lucas puts his arm around her. I just stare dumbly. At the time I was scared and concerned, but the me on TV just sits there like a lump, while Lucas helps. "Help her, you idiot," I mumble under my breath, ashamed of that man's inaction.

Lacey keeps talking as Gabby gets up and stares off across the field, the camera zooms in trying to get a view of her face. She looks slumped and beaten, a tiny quiver in her chin.

Gabby straightens her shoulders, raises her chin. The quiver disappears.

The scene cuts to Gabby by her car, Lacey hounding her and Gabby trying to escape.

"This woman has nothing to do with our investigation," I tell the camera.

"Apparently local *psychic* Gabriella McAllister failed to help the police in their investigation today. She did put on a good show, though," Lacey says. "Stay tuned as we follow this story once actual details from the police become available.

The show cuts to commercial and I stab the off button.

"That wasn't much of a news story, more of an attack piece on Gabby. How can Lacey call herself a journalist?" I throw the remote on the side table with a clatter.

Alexis raises her eyebrows. "Sensational journalism sells, I guess. She should have spent more time talking to you, getting the real story."

I push down the recliner part and put my elbows on my knees. "She was right, though."

"Who, Lacey?"

"No, Gabby was right. Everything she said she saw in her vision was right. The ME report came back and everything else we have learned today matches." I stare at the carpet below my feet avoiding looking at Alexis.

"So it's real?"

I nod at the carpet. "It's always been real." I hang my head even lower. The picture of my sister standing in that field, looking defeated before raising her chin to face us replays in a loop in my head.

"But, I thought…."

"I know, so did I." I squeeze my wife's knee. "Look, I need to go talk to her. We kind of got into it earlier and I was a jerk."

Alexis flashes me a look of surprise, then hides it. "Of course, if you need to."

I kiss her on the cheek, then go before I lose my nerve.


I haven't been to Gabby's house since five years ago when I helped her move in. Grandma Dot made me help her. I've driven by it on patrol, but have never stopped by to visit. It sits in the part of town built in the 50's, in a line of similar small houses and large trees. It's only a few blocks from the home we grew up in. I try to avoid both houses if at all possible.

Gabby's house has two windows on the front, a stoop and door between them. A one-car garage was added on the side at some point, apparently by someone who didn't know what they were doing. The roof sags and the door hangs at an odd angle. The door must not work right, because Gabby's navy blue Charger is parked in the driveway instead of in the garage.

The tension in my shoulders clamps with a vengeance as I stand on her front stoop. I toe at the weeds growing in the cracks of the concrete steps. I inspect the peeling paint of the door, flick a piece of it off with my thumbnail while I stall.

I've faced drug dealers and armed robbers, but somehow knocking on my sister's door fills me with dread. Disgusted with myself, I raise my fist and knock louder than I intended. The sound echoes across the yard in a sharp report.

She takes forever to answer and it annoys me. I know she's home, her car is here, the lights are on. It's too early for her to be in bed. My annoyance climbs, when finally the door opens just a crack and she peeks out.

"Dustin? What are you doing here?" Her weary voice slides through the crack in the door that she doesn't open wider.

"Can we talk?"

The door shuts in my face, not hard but shut. Anger flares in my belly, until I hear the unmistakable sound of the door chain being unlocked. Light pours onto the stoop as she opens the door wide and steps back.

"I guess I can't say no, so come on in."

Her house is neat and efficient. Living room on the left, eat-in kitchen on the right, two bedrooms and a bath in back. It's basically a box with four boxes inside it. Her whole house could fit in my open concept kitchen and great room at home.

Gabby goes to a side table by the front door, and picks up her gloves. "You don't need to do that," I say.

She doesn't seem to believe me, but drops the gloves anyway. "You want something to drink?" The whole thing feels awkward and uncomfortable, so we fall back on politeness.

"Sure. Do you have any sweet tea?"

She makes a nervous sound almost like a giggle. "Of course." Growing up with Grandma Dot meant lots of tea, not just her herbal blends, but sweet tea by the jug with lots of sugar.

Gabby switches on the light in the kitchen revealing almost empty counters, and very little decorations. Looking around, the whole house seems stark and empty.

None of the personal items most houses accumulate. I decide not to comment on it.

She hands me the tea and holds her own glass. We stand in the kitchen, awkward silence stretching around us. My mouth feels dry suddenly and I take a sip.

"Did you really drive all the way over here to drink tea in my kitchen and just stand there?" Her snappy tone frustrates me, but that's okay. Being frustrated with her is familiar, I can work with that.

"I came to talk to you. Can we sit down?"

Gabby huffs past me and flops down on the couch. She must not have many visitors, because there is nowhere else to sit unless I want to sit on the couch with her. I lean against the door jamb instead.

"So talk." She stares at the TV, even though the screen is blank.

"Did you see the news today?" Now that I'm here, I don't know where to start.

She pulls a yellow blanket tight around her and shrinks farther into the couch. "Lacey made me look like a psycho. I don't know why she hates me so much."

"Forget Lacey." I take another sip of the tea, then plow on. "I got the medical examiner's report back."

This draws her attention away from the blank TV. "What did it say?"

"The same thing you said. The age of the bones, the age and sex of the victim are all consistent with what you saw. We are testing DNA against the sons of Karen Jennings, but I feel confident that you were right."

Her posture softens and she loosens her grip on the

blanket. She looks like the little sister I remember from years ago, looking at me for approval.

"So you don't think I'm crazy?" The need in her hopeful words burns.

"I've never thought you were crazy." I came here to talk to her, to be honest.

"What about earlier, at Grandma's?" I'd hoped she'd let me off easy, no such luck. Shame at flinching away from her swims in my belly.

"I'm sorry about that. I don't know what I was thinking."

"You were thinking I was a monster. I saw it on your face." She turns back to the blank TV, pulls the blanket tight around her again.

"You're not a monster, Gabby, but the truth is you freak me out." She narrows her eyes and looks at me, but doesn't say anything. I push on. "I've never understood any of this 'gift' stuff. You and Grandma act like it's some special club you belong to and I am always the outsider. Honestly, I thought it was a bunch of crap. That you were just doing it for attention." Her eyes get even narrower, her lips pursed into a tight line.

"I've never made it up for attention. I didn't ask for it, I don't even want it." The venom drips from her simple words.

"Today was real. And, yeah, it scared me, I admit it. I don't know what else to tell you." The honesty must have worked because her eyes go back to normal and her mouth relaxes. The silence hangs heavy between us, though.

Suddenly a blur of gray and white fur jumps out from under the couch and onto Gabby's lap. Instinctively, I reach for my gun, although I don't have it with me. The cat settles on her lap and she strokes it without thinking. I almost laugh at the absurdity of my reaction.

"It's just Chester. You don't need to shoot him," she says.

"See, like that. You know things and say things that are, I don't know, freaky."

"You're a cop, you were startled. You reached for your hip where your gun would be. I don't need *powers* to make the connection." She laughs suddenly, the quick change of mood unsettling. "Remember the cat we had growing up? That huge white fluffy thing?"

"I remember. We called him Blanco. That cat sucked." I cross the room and sit on the far end of the couch.

"Dad brought it home, said he found it in a parking lot somewhere. Remember how bad he smelled, and Mom tried to give him a bath?"

"And he tore her arms up and hid under the couch for hours. That cat hated us. Never let anyone except Dad pet him." We sit quietly together, remembering. Those days feel like shimmery memories of an old movie, not like our life.

"What happened?" I finally get the nerve up to ask the question I have wanted to ask for thirteen years.

"I think he ran away or something."

"No, I mean, what happened, that night? I've never asked you." If this is a night for honesty, I'm going for the big questions.

71

"I don't remember. Honest, I don't." I know she's telling the truth, but it isn't enough. Gabby unknowingly rubs the scar on her eyebrow.

"You have to remember something. You were there when she did it."

"She didn't do it!" The words are nearly a scream and I flinch involuntarily. "I don't remember what happened, but I know Mom didn't do that to Dad. I just know."

This isn't going well, and I wish I hadn't brought it up. We've managed to avoid the topic for years, I should have left it that way.

"But she's in prison. I've seen the file, everything points to her. She had a trial, and was convicted." The words are bitter on my tongue. I want Mom to be innocent too, but no matter how I turn it in my mind, I can't come to any other conclusion.

"They never found his body." She clings to the words as she has clung to our mother's innocence. Gabby visits her once a month at the women's prison in Indianapolis. I haven't seen my mother since the trial. As far as I'm concerned, she is dead too. But sometimes, like tonight, the doubts get to me.

"He could still be alive out there, somewhere." Gabby looks tiny and fragile curled in the corner of the couch. A lost little girl, who wants her daddy.

"Maybe." I take pity on her, let her have her hope. I don't cling to hope anymore. The first few years after it happened, hope was all I had. I prayed every night he would come home, that the murder was all a big mistake.

After a while, I quit praying. I learned to focus on

facts.

Gifts and powers and a magical return of a murdered father were Gabby's way of dealing, not mine.

"Why did you come here, Dustin? We've never been close, that's how we work. Why all the questions tonight?"

I'm thinking about my answer to that. The image of her standing in that field, lifting her chin plays through my mind again. Why did I come? Some latent brotherly love thing? She is more upset now than when I got here. Before I can form an answer, a nearby dog starts barking, deep and insistent. "You don't have a dog too, do you?"

"No, that's the neighbor's dog. He's kind of annoying."

The barking continues, the insistence of it catching my cop attention. Laughter and shuffling sounds from outside make me spring across the few steps to her front door. "Hey you!" I shout as I throw the door open.

Two shadowy figures lurk by Gabby's garage. My shout and sudden appearance chases them off.

"Gabby, do you have a front light?"

"What's going on?" She switches on a porch light, it does nothing to illuminate the garage door.

I get a flashlight out of the glove box of my personal car and wish I had driven the cruiser. No one will vandalize a house with a cop car in the driveway.

Gabby huddles next to me, the beam of the flashlight shining on the one word they managed to paint before I chased them off. The red spray paint on the white of the door stands out even in the dull beam of the flashlight.

73

FREAK.

"Welcome to my world." Gabby sounds tired, but not surprised. Her accepting manner angers me more than the vandalism.

"Has this happened before?"

"Let's just say, I have a large container of paint remover, and I've gotten good at using it."

# Chapter 8

## GABBY

Dustin's visit shakes me more than the vandalism. It's not the first time punks have done something to my house. After convincing Dustin I will clean it up tomorrow, I get him to leave. I know he came here meaning to be helpful, to heal our relationship, but really he just confused me. At least he finally admitted he believed in my gift and I wasn't a monster. That part soothes, but dragging up the mess with Mom and Dad diluted any progress we made.

Curled up on the couch, Chester purring in my lap, the memories I have so diligently buried rise to the surface. Impressions mostly, more like the visions I have than actual memories. Most times I trick myself, believe they belong to someone else.

Dustin had been at his friend's that night. I'd been in my room reading, lost in a book, not paying attention. Mom and Dad were fighting about something. The usual kind of fighting that popped up occasionally, nothing special. I didn't even listen to the words.

The front door slammed and I heard Mom's car leave.

I heard her leave. I'm sure of it.

I got to the end of my chapter and went out to the kitchen for a snack before bed. Dad was there, loading the dishwasher, setting up the coffee maker for the morning. Doing the usual things I had seen him do a hundred times before. He was maybe a little more tense than normal, but not unduly upset.

"Hey, kiddo, want some ice cream?" he asked, totally normal.

"You know it." He got out two bowls, one scoop in each. We sat at the bar in the kitchen, talked about the silly things fourteen-year-old girls talk about. It was just another night. I didn't ask where Mom went.

I should have asked.

We finished the ice cream and he put the bowls in the dishwasher. "I'm gonna go read some more and go to bed," I said. I kissed his cheek, gave him a quick hug the way I'd done a hundred times before.

I wish I had held him tight, had clung longer.

I never saw my dad again.

I read for a while, and didn't hear Mom come home. That's what I told the detectives later, I never heard her come home. I fell asleep with the book in my hand.

Sometime later, I woke to crashing.

Loud, continuous crashing, not a 'single plate dropped in the kitchen' kind of sound. Instantly awake, terror flooded my body, held me frozen in bed. I listened to the battle raging on the other side of my bedroom wall. Muffled cries and shouts of rage seeped through the wall. Men's voices, not my mom's. I told the detectives that too, but they didn't listen.

A few moments later, everything went quiet. The lack of sound was more terrifying than the crashing.

I forced myself out of bed, crept to my door. Pressing my ear to the wood, I listened intently.

Nothing.

I turned the knob and cracked the door open, peered down the hall.

Still nothing.

Shadows drenched the end of the hall. The eerie quiet hung in the air. I took a tentative step towards the kitchen, then another. The air smelled different, not like my house. It rankled my nose and I blew air out hard to remove the smell.

I reached the end of the hall, strained to see in the darkness. The lights were off. I told them that too. If Mom had been home, the lights would have been on.

I reached for the switch around the corner. A sound caught my attention before I could flip the switch.

"Dad?" I tried to say.

Pain smashed into my face, hitting me at the eyebrow.

Searing pain, stabbing my brain.

I floated in light for a long time.

Bright, enveloping light. Nothing but light. There wasn't a tunnel like they say on TV. No one called my name. It was just white light, beautiful and pure. The light felt like home, true home. I never wanted to leave.

But my eyes eventually opened.

Grandma Dot's worried face greeted me. Dustin slouched in a chair across the room. The room was bright, but nothing like the light I just left. Leaving that light tore at my heart. I desperately wanted to go back to the pureness of it. I needed the light.

Instead, I woke in a hospital bed with three stitches in my eyebrow and a headache that wouldn't quit. My entire world was shattered and I knew it.

I screamed when I awoke.

I screamed and I cried. No amount of comforting from Grandma Dot could soothe me.

"Dad, where are you?!" I screamed. "I want my mom! Where's my mom?"

I already knew what they were going to tell me.

I wanted the light, the pure peaceful light. I was given a different kind of light instead.

From that day on, I knew lots of things I shouldn't know.

But I never would know the one thing I desperately needed.

What happened in that kitchen?


Luckily the alarm on my phone is preset, because I wake up on the couch stiff and groggy. I punch the screen to make the alarm stop. Chester realizes I'm awake and jumps on me. Any hope I had for fading back to sleep and ignoring the day ahead was dashed by his insistent attention. I forgot to feed him last night, I'm amazed he let me sleep.

I fill his dish and flip on the TV out of habit. Lacey Aniston's voice shakes me fully awake. "Developing information on the case of the bones found yesterday. A source tells us the bones are the remains of Karen Jennings who was thought to have left town with one Steven Rawlings twenty years ago. Both Jennings and Rawlings had plans to leave together and were never heard from again. With the remains of Karen Jennings found, the question now is where is Steven Rawlings?"

I punch off the TV in disgust. Lacey should be ashamed of herself. Rumors and speculation are not news.

Her question nags, though. Where is Steven Rawlings? If he was running off with Karen, and Karen never left, then what happened to Steven? Did he kill her then skip town as Lacey seemed to imply?


I ignore the "FREAK" spray painted on my crooked garage door and head to work on the other side of town. The building is remarkable only in its plainness. The flat roof, evenly spaced windows and orange colored bricks, look like any other office building. The cracked asphalt parking lot with weeds tufting up adds to the overall depressing mood of the place. Small, stenciled letters on the entry door, "Customer Clearinghouse," is the only advertisement.

Inside, it's more of the same generic look. Fake plants sit by the door, a failed attempt at a welcome. Cubicles run in neat rows, each filled with a customer service agent with a headset, computer screen and a forced positive attitude.

Customer Clearinghouse takes call-in orders for several catalog companies. Even in the age of the internet, a surprising number of people still like to call in orders from catalogs they receive in the mail. You never know if the next caller wants to order pet supplies, or clothes, or "adult" items, depending on which catalog they are calling about.

I duck my head and try to sneak past my boss's office. It doesn't work.

"Gabby, there you are." Herbert Zenderman's voice has an unusual edge of interest to it. "Come in here. I want to talk to you."

Herbert's normally pale, thin face flushes as I stand in front of his desk. "Sorry about calling in at the last minute yesterday," I start to apologize.

He fans the air with sharp erratic waves of his hand. "Never mind that. I saw you on the news last night. Is it true?" He practically crackles with excitement.

"I was on the news, that's true," I answer vaguely.

He leans forward, lowers his voice in a conspiratorial way. "I mean, is it true you got a psychic reading on some bones?" His honest interest, not fear, surprises me.

"I'm not psychic. I can't tell the future or anything. But I do sense things sometimes."

"And you touched the bones? What did you see? In the video, it looked like you saw something." His obvious hunger for a juicy story makes me feel sorry for him.

"I did see something, but I'm not supposed to talk about it."

"Wow. Amazing." He sits back in his chair, looks at me like I am a celebrity or something. I suppose to him I am. "It was a woman, wasn't it? And she was murdered?"

I nod. Lacey already broadcasted the information.

"Are you going to help the cops solve the case? Like the psychics do on TV?" I know he's excited, but this is too much.

"Herbert, can I just get back to work, please?"

"Yes, yes, of course." He waves his hands again, a nervous gesture. "If you need more time off or anything while you are helping the cops, just let me know. This is so cool."

I just manage to keep my eyes from rolling.

I slink down the third aisle to my cubicle on the end. Dozens of one-sided conversations swirl around me. A few coworkers flash me odd looks. My friend, Haley, works in the cubicle next to mine. She catches my eye as I pass.

"One moment, let me look that up for you," she says to a customer on her head set, then hits the mute button.

"I saw you on the news last night. Wow!" she says to me. "We gotta talk on break." Haley hits the mute button again and goes back to helping her customer.

I don't mind Haley's interest. She's the closest thing I have to a friend. I don't trust the other coworkers. I feel

81

eyes on me from around the room, and a few whispered side-comments. Lacey's stupid "sensational news" story has made me the talk of the town.

I slip on my headset and focus on work. None of the callers know who I am or what I did yesterday. I'm just an anonymous voice selling things.

# Chapter 9

## GABBY

I'm feeling good when I pull into my driveway after work. Haley had grilled me good-naturedly during break about my work with the bones. Her open fascination rubbed off on the other co-workers. Curious faces gathered around me at lunch, wanting to hear the story too. I'm not used to that much attention, at least not positive attention.

The "FREAK" on my garage door shatters my good mood.

The paint remover softens the letters, and the red swirls under my rag. I should have gotten to it earlier, before it cured. I keep scrubbing, but a faint red haze remains. I'll either have to re-paint the door or live with the smudges.

In frustration, I throw the rag at the trash can near the corner of the garage. It doesn't even come close, slaps on the concrete with a sick sound. I stomp to the rag, throw it in the trash, and slam the lid down hard.

"Whoa, what did that trash can ever do to you?" Preston laughs at me from his driveway next door. I didn't even know he was standing there, I was so caught up in my anger at the paint. I feel violated, being watched like that, but also oddly flattered.

"I'm not mad at the trash can," I mumble.

"I saw what they wrote, the jerks. Looks like you got it off now." He's trying to cheer me up, acts as if nasty graffiti is normal. I'm ashamed he saw it at all and don't know what to say.

"So, hey," he walks a few steps closer. "I got free passes to the big Corn Maze for Friday." Preston looks away across the yards, across the street.

"That sounds fun." I toe the wet mark on the concrete left by the rag.

"The car dealership where I work is giving out free passes as a promotion," he hedges.

"Preston, are you asking me out?" I smile, hoping I didn't misread the situation.

"I'm trying to." His smile meets mine. "I know it's just the Corn Maze, but it sounds fun. I've never been."

"Sounds great. I'd love to go." His shoulders loosen. His obvious relief at my acceptance almost makes me laugh. I just washed "FREAK" off my garage after all.

84

Between Preston asking me out and the acceptance I received at work, I should be in a good mood. Tense, edgy energy pumps through me. Random adrenaline spikes flutter in my chest. I flit between cleaning my apartment and trying to focus on TV.

Memories of the dead woman in the field intrude. Questions about the missing man swirl.

Who killed Karen? Did Steven do it and take off? Did her husband kill her instead of letting her go? The husband is always the first suspect, but the vision didn't line up with that theory.

My thoughts tangle and confuse. The house tightens around me. I toy with the idea of going to the superstore to people-watch, but I can't sit still that long.

I rub the cross tattoo on my inner forearm, trying to center myself. I got the tattoo not long after the basketball game fire incident. I wasn't technically old enough for a tattoo, but Grandma Dot signed for it, and understood how important it was to me. It represents everything I lost, everything I gained. It's a mark that I nearly died, maybe actually did die, and that God saved me for a reason.

The tattoo doesn't buzz.

I'm jumpy anyway.

Thinking a run might calm my jangled nerves, I tie on my running shoes and grab a jacket against the overcast October sky. The park by the river is deserted, my Charger the only car in the lot. Suddenly, I don't feel like running. I drive a lap through the parking lot and get back on the road. I can't stop thinking about Karen, about the missing Steven. I turn right out of the parking lot, the opposite direction from home.

The field that was Karen Jennings' grave feels eerie in the fading darkness. The bulldozer hasn't moved since yesterday. The crime scene tape flaps in the rising breeze. Houses from the neighborhood on the other side of the tree line shine with families going about their daily routines. One of those houses belongs to Dustin, but I can't tell which one from here. The lights in the houses glow warm and welcoming.

I sit alone in my car.

A large drop of rain splatters on my windshield, runs down the glass in slow motion. I flick the wipers on and they streak across the windshield with a squeal. I'm not quite sure why I came here, so I watch the rain drip down the windshield and listen to the wind.

I rub my tattoo. It still hasn't tingled, which surprises me.

"Crap on a cracker, Gabby. You drove out here for a reason. Just get out of the car." My voice echoes against the windshield. I climb out before I can change my mind.

The raising breeze catches the car door, slams it hard. The sound startles me. A nervous crack of laughter escapes my lips. The cold seeps down my collar, a few drops of drizzle roll down my cheeks. Wishing I had worn a heavier jacket, I pull the collar tighter.

Karen's bones are no longer here, but I feel the buzz anyway.

I lift the wet plastic crime scene tape and duck under.

The place where Karen had lain for more than 20 years yawns open, a black mouth in the moonlight. I crouch next to the dirt, and take off my glove. The cold bites my bare skin. "God, let me see what I need to see," I say my usual prayer. Before I lose my nerve, I place my bare hand on the dirt where her bones were, and close my eyes.

Nothing, just dirt.

I sit back on my heels, confused, sure I would see something new. The area still buzzes around me, but I can't get a reading. I touch the dirt again, hoping for a new clue.

Still nothing.

Disappointment swirls in my gut.

My tattoo finally wakes up to the situation and tingles the familiar sign.

I stand in the dark, listen to the wind, listen to the small, still voice in my head that leads me. The buzz grows stronger. From the nearby neighborhood, a dog barks. Two sharp sounds in the dark. I back away from the dirt, turn my head side to side, trying to get a direction on the buzz.

Sharp metal pokes me in the back. I jump, turning on my attacker. The wind swallows my startled scream.

The bulldozer hulks behind me.

Nervous laughter bubbles up, overtakes me. I throw my head back and I laugh like a crazy person into the wind. Alone at a crime scene, screaming at a bulldozer in the dark, maybe I am crazy.

I lean against the machine to catch my breath, my left hand against the cold metal.

The shock from the machine makes my hand snatch away.

My crazy laughter stops cold.

The buzz rings in my ears.

I stretch out my hand again, touch the machine.

*He's under the bulldozer.*

I fall to my hands and knees next to the massive tracks of the machine.

I touch the grass.

He calls out to me through the dirt. I feel him under the ground, aching to be found.

I can't actually touch him, so I don't get a clear vision, but I am sure.

I've found Steven Rawlings.

# Chapter 10

## GABBY

The drizzling rain starts again, dripping down the collar of my jacket in cold rivulets. I kneel in the grass next to the bulldozer, the dampness soaking into the knees of my running leggings.

Steven calls out to me, trying to communicate. He's out of reach, buried under where the bulldozer sits. I should call someone, and I will. But for now, I sit alone with the dead man. A victim, not the killer.

I lay flat on the damp grass, face down. The smell of earth fills my nose, the primal scent a perfect fit for the situation. I need to be closer to him.

I wriggle until my body pushes against the muddy tracks of the dozer. There's an opening just large enough for my arm to fit through. I push my left hand under the machine, reaching for Steven. The dry grass crinkles under my palm, protected from the rain.

I stretch as close as I can without being able to move the dozer.

It will have to be enough.

I open my mind, invite him in. My body yearns to pull away, to go home. I face the fear. I might live through his death in my mind, but I need to know.

The images shimmer, like wavy watercolor paintings. Images similar to Karen's vision.

*Excitement about leaving, a knock on the door, someone familiar.*

At first I think I'm just seeing Karen again.

*Fear for his daughter. Hurry. Sharp blade, betrayal. Pain. Then darkness.*

Although muted, the emotion of the vision slams into me. The pain, the confusion, the final slip into death overwhelms me.

My body screams to pull my hand away, but I force it to stay.

The vision replays, and I focus as hard as I can, trying to see something new. The blade sliding into his flesh stabs my own chest. The sick slip into darkness pulls me with it.

My body finally wins. I roll away from the dozer in a frenzy of fear. My arm barely fits through the gap in the track. The back of my hand catches on a piece of metal, scraping a stinging line down my skin.

I suck the blood from the scratch, the metal taste

mixing with the scent of the machine. The small sting is nothing compared to the stabbing in the vision.

I lay in the dirt and grass and cry for the loss of the man buried below the dozer. The rain comes down in earnest now, splashes on my face, mixes with my tears. Sobs tear at my chest, and a keening wail rides on the wind.

The dog in the neighborhood barks in response.

The cold and rain finally pull me from my private torture. I stumble shivering to my car, and slide into the worn leather seat. I blast the heat, focus on the sound of the rain pounding on the roof.

I need to call someone, tell them what I found.

The line of houses from the neighborhood nearby twinkle through the wet windshield. Dustin is there now, close. I hold my phone in my clammy hand, debating. Dustin could be here in a few minutes.

I dial Lucas's number.

"Hey, Gabby." He sounds pleased to hear from me, not surprised. His voice warms me more than the heat blasting out of the dash.

"Lucas?" One word, just his name.

"What's wrong?" Instant concern.

"I found Steven Rawlings," I sniffle. He doesn't ask me how, bless him.

"Where are you?" He's all action now. I imagine him, grabbing his things, getting ready to come to me.

"Where you found Karen. He's under the bulldozer."

The silence of unasked questions.

His voice sounds tired when he finally talks again.

"Don't move. I'll be right there."

Lucas' cruiser pulls in behind my Charger. No lights, no sirens. He turns off his headlights too. My windows have fogged over, and I don't see him approach. He pulls the passenger door open and slides in, out of the rain.

"Are you okay?" The question surprises me. I expected him to be mad. The kindness breaks me.

"Not really," my voice catches and I fight a new batch of tears.

Lucas gathers me against him. The gear shifter digs into my leg as I lean over, but his arms around me are strong, protective. I give in to the comfort, for just a few moments, and manage to keep the tears away.

Stronger now, I sit up, watch the rain.

"So, what happened?" he asks.

I tell him the basics of how I found him, not sure he'll believe me. I leave out the part about laying in the rain, crying in fear.

"You're sure it's Steven?"

"Yeah." My voice sounds far away, someone else's.

"Did you, you know, see anything?"

"Basically the same thing I saw with Karen. He was going to leave, someone he knew came to his house. He was worried about his daughter and went with them. The killer must have tricked them both. Karen was worried about her boys, Steven about his daughter. The killer must have used the kids being hurt as a way to get them into the car with them."

Lucas thinks about this for a while. "That would work

92

to lure them out. If I thought something happened to Olivia, I would go, let down my guard. A shitty thing to do, though."

"So is murder," I say gently. "We're not dealing with a nice guy here."

"Is it a guy? The killer? Did you see something new this time?" He sounds so hopeful, I hate to dash it.

"No. I guess I shouldn't have said guy. Could be a woman. I have no idea."

We listen to the rain and the wipers. In another time and place, sitting here together would feel homey and safe.

"I've gotta call this in. God knows how I'm going to explain it."

"I could call in an anonymous tip," I suggest.

"There's no way you can make this anonymous. Everyone will know it's you. Who else could find a body hidden under a bulldozer?" He thinks for a moment. "Under the dozer. We never moved it, left the scene just as we found it." He sounds disgusted.

"You had no way to know there was another body out there."

"You knew."

"I didn't know. I just came here to…. I don't know why I came here. I just did," I finish lamely.

Lucas runs his hands through his hair, agitated. "Crap!" His voice rings through the car. Guilt stabs me fast.

"I'm sorry, Lucas. I never expected to find another body. Especially like this."

He blows out air, exasperated. "Don't be sorry, Gabby. I'm the one who pulled you into this thing in the first place. I'll call Dustin and tell him what's going on. You go home. I'll take care of it."

"But, what are you going to tell him?"

"The only thing I can, the truth. Now go home and get a shower. You're covered in mud."

Lucas climbs out of our little universe and into the rain. I hate that he's upset, but I am not sorry I found Steven. The man needed to be found, and if that makes life complicated for me, then so be it.


I expected the phone to ring at some point in the night. Expected Dustin to berate me about going to the crime scene. I expect a bunch of questions I don't want to answer.

What I didn't expect was to sleep soundly through the night. No missed calls, no texts on my phone. Was the whole thing a dream?

My muddy and grassy clothes piled where I left them on the bathroom floor, proves last night really happened.

With a cringe, I turn on the morning news. During my second cup of coffee, the story finally plays. A different reporter, not Lacey Aniston, explains that more remains have been found and they are suspected to be Steven Rawlings. No mention of me or how they were found. I'm not sure what magic Lucas used to keep me out of it, but thank God for small miracles.

On my way to work, I drive past the crime scene. Last

night's rain has blown over and the construction site looks less imposing in the morning sun. I don't pull in, just drive by slowly. The bulldozer has been moved and a crew works where it sat last night. The area crawls with official vehicles and police. In the distance, I see Lucas, still in the street clothes he had on last night. He looks haggard, but in his element. Closer to the road, a uniformed officer has his back to me. Hearing me driving slowly, the man looks over his shoulder. I lock eyes with Dustin, the anger in his face evident, even from the road. I hit the gas and speed away, feeling guilty.

I try to slink to my cubicle, the same way I did yesterday. Herbert catches me again, full of questions about the newest development.

"Did you have anything to do with the new body being found?" he asks. He's so excited to have something interesting happening in our boring workplace. I feel sorry for him, but I lie anyway.

"Sorry, wasn't me."

His face falls, no doubt disappointed he won't have any new stories to tell his friends.

Just after lunch, his prospects for gossip turn better. I'm in the middle of helping a woman choose which color of bedspread she wants to order, and I don't see him approach. Herbert taps me on the shoulder and I let out a little yelp. The woman on the line doesn't notice, just keeps talking, more to herself than to me. Herbert motions to the front door where a slight man with short clipped red curls watches me with interest. I nod to Herbert and wrap up the call with my customer.

The man watches me with curious intensity as I approach him standing near the fake plants by the front door. A little niggle stirs in the back of my mind and slows my steps.

"Are you Gabby McAllister?" His face holds a haunted look, a touch of fear he tries to hide. I nod.

"I'm Seth Jennings. Karen Jennings was my mother. Can we talk somewhere?" The words pour out quickly, like he needs to say them before he loses his nerve.

"There's a bench outside. Let's sit out there."

# Chapter 11

## GABBY

The blue sky stretches overhead and silence stretches between us on the bench. I saw this man's mother die, what can I say to him that doesn't sound awkward?

"Your grandma told me where to find you," he finally says, focusing on the cars in the parking lot, not on me.

"She told me you boys and your father get your hair cut there," I say to fill the space.

Seth Jennings stares at the cars like they will drive away if he takes his eyes off them. The October sun does little to chase the chill away and I wish he would get to his point. I decide to help him along.

"Mr. Jennings, what can I do for you?"

He looks away from the cars and towards me, his eyes

brushing as far as my knees, not up to my face. He's afraid of me. I've seen this dance before.

"You don't have to be afraid of me. I don't bite."

A nervous bark of laughter, low and sad.

"I know that. It's just-. They say you saw my mother, in a vision or something, is that true?"

"I did." Simple truth usually goes far.

"Wha-, what did you see?" He looks me full in the face now, his need to know stronger than his fear of me.

"Her last thoughts were of you and your brother." His face pulls in, a grimace of pain. It dawns on me this man spent the last twenty years thinking his mom ran off with a boyfriend and forgot about him. I can't imagine the pain dredged up by the change in story, even with all my powers.

"Whoever took her told her you and your brother-, I'm sorry, I don't know his name."

"Nicholas."

"They told her you and Nicholas were hurt and tricked her into their car. All she wanted was to get to you. Then, you know, she couldn't."

Seth Jennings hangs his head, fighting the emotion.

"So she wasn't going to leave us?" He sounds like the little boy he was then, the hope so raw in his voice. I hate to crush it, but I have to tell the truth.

"She was going to leave." Again simple truths.

The boy inside him grows up before my eyes. His back stiffens, his chin rises.

He asks the obvious question. "My dad didn't kill her, did he?"

98

"No. It was someone she trusted, but I don't think it was your dad."

"And the boyfriend, Steven Rawlings that they just found?"

"I don't know much about that," I hedge. "But, it was the same killer. Not your dad."

Seth thinks about this for a while, back to holding the cars in place in the parking lot with his gaze.

"Will you help me?"

"I'm not sure what I can do to help."

"They haven't come out and said it yet, but my dad will be the first one they think did it. They were found on our land, his wife and her boyfriend." That word said with heavy sarcasm. "Dad didn't do it. I knew that before you told me. But it won't take long until they come after him."

This thought had already crossed my mind. "Mr. Jennings, where is your father? Why isn't he asking me this?"

"He had a stroke this summer. It destroyed most of his mind. He's in the nursing home now. That's why we sold the farm to the developer. He's very fragile now. He won't live through an investigation, a trial. God forbid they find him guilty, he'll die in prison. I can't let that happen."

Full eye contact now, his loyalty burning bright in his eyes. I've seen the same look in my own eyes, every time I visit my mother in prison. Another innocent doomed by circumstances.

"I'll do what I can, but I'm not the police, I don't have any real weight in this."

"Your brother's in charge of the investigation."

"Dustin doesn't really listen to me," I scoff.

"I can pay you. You're all I have."

As a rule, I don't touch people, but I reach for his hand. He doesn't pull away from me, allows the small squeeze.

"Let's start by talking to your dad."

Herbert gives me the rest of the day off without asking questions. I know he'll grill me tomorrow for details, but at least he lets me go.

I've never been to a nursing home before, my expectations colored by scenes on TV. I make sure my gloves are on tight and follow Seth into Life Village. Constructed just a few years ago, Life Village looks more like a mid-grade hotel lobby than the homes I've seen on TV. The smell of disinfectant and the lingering sense of sadness contrasts with the neutral colored décor and artwork.

Seth checks us into the front desk and we find Patrick Jennings in the day room. The man doesn't look old enough to be in a nursing home. Some quick math puts his age in his sixties, nowhere near old enough to need full-time care. Even from across the room, the damage from the stroke is obvious. He sits in a wheelchair parked at an odd angle to the room. His head slumps slightly to the right and he stares at the floor. Patrick should be in the prime of his life, instead he's confined to the prison of his injured brain. Now he's a murder suspect. Any doubts I had about helping clear this man's name vanish. He

100

cannot go to prison for something he didn't do.

"Dad," Seth crouches by his father's chair. "I brought someone to see you." The tenderness in his voice and the gentle way he touches his father's hand touches my heart.

I crouch next to Seth so I can look into Patrick's face.

Patrick raises his head, focuses on Seth, and delight fills his face. Then he looks at me, confused.

"This is Gabby McAllister, Dad. She's here to help us."

"Does he understand what's happened with your mother and Steven?" Patrick flinches and I take that as a yes.

"Didn't kill her," Patrick mumbles, defensive even in his weakness.

"I know you didn't, Patrick. That's why I came to see you."

"I thought she left with that man. I had no idea she was dead."

"I know, Dad. We all thought that," Seth soothes.

Suddenly, I have no idea what I should do. This is way out of my usual life. I think about what Lucas might do and start with the basics.

"Patrick, what do you remember from the night Karen disappeared?" I hope the man is lucid enough to remember a night twenty years ago. Of course, it's something he's probably thought about over and over.

"I coached the boy's baseball team back then. We were at a game. Karen normally came to watch, but that night she said she wasn't feeling well and stayed home." Patrick seems to gain strength telling the story. "We lost the game, 7-5," he trails off.

A few other residents sit in the day room, I can tell they are listening to us, but pretending they're not.

"What happened after the game?" I prompt him.

"The boys and I went home. Karen was gone. She had written a note and left it on our dresser. A note." He spits the word out. "Fourteen years of marriage, two children together and she leaves me a note that she ran off with that man." All these years later, the memory obviously burns.

"She didn't take her bag with her," I point out.

Patrick and Seth look at me, surprised I knew that.

"No she didn't. It was open on our bed, half packed."

"Didn't you think it was odd she didn't take her bag?"

Seth shoots me an angry look.

"I didn't think about it at the time. Maybe she decided to leave it behind and get all new stuff. The same way she left us behind for a new life." Patrick looks visibly tired now, the memories wearing him out.

"Did you see your mom after the baseball game?" I ask Seth.

"No. We never saw her again."

"You're sure she wasn't home?"

The angry look again. "Look, you already said you know Dad didn't do it, what's with all these questions?"

"The police are going to ask the same things. They don't have the information I have from my visions. I've told them, but they're going to lean a lot more towards the facts than my impressions. You have to be ready for the questions and have good solid answers."

102

Seth nods, resigned.

"Patrick has an alibi with the baseball game. But nothing says she wasn't home when you guys got back. He could have killed her later that night and then killed Steven too."

Seth and Patrick both make protest noises.

"We know that isn't what happened, but the police will see it that way."

A movement on the far side of the day room catches my eye and I turn involuntarily. Dustin and Lucas stand in the doorway, wearing nearly identical angry expressions. Dustin's leans more towards disgusted anger and Lucas more like concerned anger.

"I've gotta get out of here," I say quickly to Seth. I don't wait for his reply, just hurry past Dustin and Lucas. Together they fill most of the doorway. I keep my eyes down and scoot past on Lucas's side, hoping he won't stop me.

He steps aside to let me pass. "Gabby?"

I focus on the tile floor and keep walking.

Quick steps take me down the hallway towards the front entrance. I push through the doors and breathe a sigh of relief.

My relief is short-lived. Lacey Aniston and her cameraman pounce on me. I consider going back inside. The home won't let Lacey and her crew film inside. I can find an out of the way place to hide until she leaves, and Dustin and Lucas leave.

"Gabriella McAllister!" Lacey practically squeals with delight at seeing me here. "Local *psychic* Gabriella

McAllister just exited the Life Village nursing home where prime suspect Patrick Jennings currently resides. Jennings is wanted in connection to the double-homicide recently unearthed on farm land he owned at the time of the murders. Gabriella, are you part of the investigation? Are you using your *powers* to prove Patrick Jennings killed his wife and her lover?"

I don't know what parts of Lacey's speech to be most angry at. The way she says psychic and powers as if they are dirty words, or the fact she keeps calling me Gabriella. Only Grandma Dot calls me by my full name.

I focus instead on what matters. The false accusations against Patrick.

"Patrick Jennings did not kill Karen or Steven Rawlings." I look straight into the camera, speak as firmly as I can.

"How do you know? Did the real killer *talk* to you? Are you working for the family?" How did Lacey put that together?

"I don't know who the real killer is, yet. I only know Patrick Jennings did not do it." I picture the broken man inside, his worried son. "I will prove it."

Too late I realize I let Lacey push my buttons and gave her exactly what she wanted. She turns her self-satisfied smile and saccharine voice on me full-blast and asks, "And how exactly will you prove it?"

I want to pounce on her, claw at her perfect makeup and break her expensive nose. I imagine pulling out her blonde extensions, the fake hair gripped in my fingers.

Instead, I mumble "No comment," and walk away, like

I should have done in the first place.

# Chapter 12

## LUCAS

I flip the page on the report on Karen Jennings' murder. The thin file bothers me. I need more information, something to go on. I've memorized every word of the reports, but nothing makes sense yet.

I push away from my desk, giving up for the night. I leave my home office, turn out the light. The case sits in the dark.

The buzzing of my phone intrudes on my sour mood.

I'm not surprised to see Gabby's number, she's consistently unexpected.

I pretend the tingle of excitement comes from possible

new info on the case.

The way she says my name puts me in protective mode.

Keys already in hand, jacket half on, I tell her to wait for me.

"Gabby McAllister will be the death of me," I mutter to myself on the drive to the crime scene.

She's a muddy mess sitting in her car. Grass clippings cling to her hair, dirt streaks her face, matching the dark smudges under her eyes. She looks pitiful, huddled in her front seat. I want to wipe the mud away, but keep my hands in my lap.

I can only imagine what horrors she has seen this time. I held her after she saw the vision of Karen and felt her tremble against me. These visions hit her hard.

She leans into me now and I pull her close. I yearn to protect her.

Her hair smells like peaches and grass. I give in to the moment, reminding myself she's like a sister to me.

She sits up suddenly and I let her go.

I focus on my job, on the dead man she found.

The car steams with heat, but Gabby shivers. I send her home. She's been through enough.

Alone at the crime scene, the bulldozer hulks in the dark. I touch the side of the machine, only feel cold metal. I touch the ground, feel only wet grass and dirt. I can't imagine what it must be like for Gabby, to feel things beyond. I shiver and not just from the cold seeping into my coat.

The body of Steven Rawlings lays below the machine.

If Gabby says he's there, then he is.

Many people, even Dustin, think she's a fake looking for attention. I've always believed her. She has suffered from the gift. Forced to wear gloves, forced away from people and close connections.

The small-minded people in town fear her. The most to hide, deride her the loudest. Psycho, freak, witch, words often connected to her name. Murderer's daughter is another favorite. Dustin's position insulates him from the worst of it. I hear it all.

The harsh words cut me, I can't imagine what they do to Gabby.

Her gift has put me in a bad spot now. How can I explain finding Steven under the dozer and still protect Gabby.

The rain dribbles as the minutes tick away in the dark.

"Make a decision, man," I speak out loud.

I call Dustin. He's my partner on this case, and I have no other option.

I watch Dustin's house from where I stand. A shadow crosses the window, and he answers on the second ring.

"It's Lucas," I skip formalities. "Gabby found Steven Rawlings."

Dustin sighs and says, "Oh crap. Where?"

"Same place as Karen. He's under the bulldozer. I'm at the scene now."

The curtain moves at Dustin's house. I raise my hand and wave, although he probably can't see me.

"Is she there too?" He says "she," not her name. The omission irks me.

"No, I sent Gabby home. She was wet and cold and upset." If I'd expected Dustin to show some brotherly concern, I would have been disappointed.

"I'll be right there."

Dustin's attitude towards his sister baffles me. I've been his partner for a long time, and would take a bullet for him as he would for me. But the way he dismisses his flesh and blood rankles. I know his mother is in prison for murdering his father. I know Gabby nearly died at her hands too and awoke with new powers. I understand that messes with your mind, I really do. But shunning Gabby, practically blaming her for what happened makes no sense.

If my sister, Andrea, were still here, I'd stand by her no matter what.

Andrea ran away a week after her eighteenth birthday, walked out on our family and never returned. Dustin actively shuns his own sister, but I'd give anything to see mine again.

Tonight is not the time to analyze Dustin's family situation. He's my best friend and partner, and we have a job to do.

Steven Rawlings deserves my full attention.

Dustin parks his cruiser next to mine then joins me at the dozer.

"Gabby said he's under here."

"Under it? How did-." He runs his hand through his hair. "Never mind, I can guess. What was she doing out here?"

"I don't know. Called somehow, I guess."

I brace for his scoff, but it doesn't come.

"Not sure how we're going to explain this," Dustin says. "Without dragging her into it."

"Yeah, I know."

"We could just back the dozer up. Start digging ourselves until we find him."

"You mean, lie about it?"

"It's not exactly lying. We say we had a hunch Steven was buried here too, so we came out to look around and we found him."

I warm to the idea. "Makes more sense than the truth." I put on an over-dramatic tone, "So, Dustin, I have a hunch Steven is buried around here somewhere."

Dustin goes along. "You know, Lucas, I do too. Let's move this dozer and dig around, see what we find." The silly play-acting relieves the tension of the situation.

"Now we just need some shovels. I have some at home. I'll walk over and get them. You move the dozer." Dustin walks a few steps, then yells over his shoulder, "He better be down there."

"He will be," I shout back. "Gabby, I hope you're right," I mutter to the sky.

Gabby is right. Several shovel-fulls later, we find the bones of Steven Rawlings right where Gabby said they would be.

When the team shows up, we receive a few odd looks about how we found the bones. No one questions us wanting to dig under the dozer. The excitement of finding the murder suspect as a victim overshadows. Gabby's name never comes up. The department focuses on the crime and the job. For now, we got away with our little deception, and kept Gabby safe.

I'm proud we kept her out of it.

Until we see her at Life Village, talking to the prime suspect. She looks startled and guilty, like a child caught sneaking a cookie. Then she runs off like a scared puppy, not a word of explanation.

Dustin and I lied to keep her out of the case, and she's put herself right in the middle of it.

Under questioning, Seth Jennings admits he's hired Gabby to help prove his father's innocence. My instinct to protect Gabby loses ground to anger. Gabby, you're going to be the death of me.

# Chapter 13

## GABBY

"Stupid, stupid, stupid." I smack the steering wheel of my Charger as I speed out of the parking lot of Life Village. Lacey got exactly what she wanted. The clip of me defiantly vowing to prove Patrick's innocence will be aired on the five o'clock news for sure. It's the kind of thing she lives for. She'll paint me in the worst possible light, make me look as crazy as possible. I only have a few hours of relative peace until the whole town knows. If I can't clear Patrick's name and find the real killer, I may have to move to China to get away from the gossip. Worse, an innocent man will go to prison.

With that sobering thought, I focus on a plan of action. What would an actual detective do? Start with the family.

I've already talked to Seth and Patrick, but there are two victims. I need to talk to the family of Steven Rawlings. Grandma Dot said his wife works at the post office.

Maybe Diane will talk to me, before she sees the news tonight.

A short, dumpy woman, Diane Rawlings looks much older than I expected. She obviously doesn't have Grandma Dot do her hair anymore. It needs to be cut badly, streaks of white and gray fade from her roots to the mouse brown ends. Grandma could easily turn that mess into something pretty if given a chance.

Deep lines on her face form a permanent expression fairly screaming "my feet hurt." Her attitude with customers at the counter matches the expression. The unkind part of me can't blame Steven for leaving this sour woman. The kinder part of me realizes she may not have been so sour back then.

Luckily no one gets in line behind me. I approach the counter and we are alone in the post office.

"Are you Diane?" I ask tentatively.

She points to her name tag. "Says here I am. Do you have something to mail?"

"I wanted to ask you a few questions."

Her eyes tighten, the creases on her face growing deeper. "About what? Let me guess, about my dead ex-husband. Well, not "ex" because since he took off and disappeared, I could never divorce him." The venom surprises me.

"Except he didn't leave," I point out.

"He was going to. He told me that morning. Said he

was running off with that tramp, Karen Jennings."

"You knew he was leaving? What did you do?"

"I took my daughter, Rachel, and went to my mother's in South Bend. Steven always had a roving eye, I lived with that. Straight up leaving me for that woman, was too much."

"So you were angry with him?"

"Of course I was." She stops and stares at me, finally realizing she is pouring her guts out to a stranger. "Wait, who are you and why all the questions?"

Crap on a cracker, she caught on.

"I'm just an interested citizen," I hedge. "Did you, or even your daughter, tell anyone about Steven planning to leave?"

"Yeah, I blabbed to the whole town my cheating husband left me. What do you think?" she replied sarcastically.

"So no one knew except you two?"

"Look, the police have already been here to question me. I don't need more crap from an 'interested citizen.' Why don't you just leave me and Rachel alone? This has been hard enough on us."

I decide to make my exit. "Thank you for your time," I say politely and turn to leave. A customer is coming in now anyway.

"Wait, you're that psychic woman on the news! What's your deal? Haven't you caused enough trouble already?" The anger directed at me makes me stop and swing back to Diane.

"I didn't cause any trouble! The killer did. Two people

115

are dead and I'm just trying to find out the truth."

Another customer comes in, a second witness to my tirade.

"You're just trying to get attention. I've heard about you. Screaming fire that time, you should be locked up."

I'm used to people being less than friendly, but outright hostility is rare. The hatred she spews hits like a slap in the face.

"If you knew anything about me, you'd know there really was a fire at the game. I saved hundreds of lives. I realize you've had a rough day with me finding your dead husband and all, so I will forgive you this time, but stay away from me from now on."

"What do you mean, you found him? The police said they did."

Crap, I didn't mean to let that fact slip. A third person now stands with the first two, watching the show with avid interest. I raise my chin, daring them to say anything and hurry out of the post office.

Moving to China sounds better and better.


Since Diane was in South Bend at the time of the murders, I am out of suspects. I need more information, and I know just the person to talk to, Grandma Dot. She got me into this mess anyway, telling Seth where to find me at work.

I call Seth on the way over and ask him to meet with me at Grandma's.

"I can be there in just a bit," Seth says.

"Seth, you probably already know this, but your dad needs a lawyer," I caution him.

"Got that covered. My brother Nicholas is an attorney in Fort Wayne. He's representing Dad."

"Can he meet with us too? I'd like to talk to him."

"He's actually on his way to River Bend now, I'll have him meet us."

I park my Charger next to Grandma's flatbed truck behind the farmhouse. The open sign on the shop is turned off, but one car remains in the public parking area. Through the large window in the kitchen, I can just make out the soft purple glow of Mrs. Mott's hairdo sitting at the table with Grandma. Fine with me. Mrs. Mott likes me and I can use all the friends I can get right now.

The familiar scents of the kitchen envelop me as I walk in the door. The tension in my shoulders fades some. Grandma's dog, Jet, bounces across the kitchen, dances for my attention. His antics make me laugh and the tension fades some more. It's good to be home.

Grandma Dot and Mrs. Mott sit at the kitchen table, cups of tea in hand. Neither seem surprised to see me. In fact, I get the distinct impression they've been waiting for me.

"Figured you'd come by sooner or later today," Grandma says as I stoop to give her a hug.

"I need tea." I chuckle.

"Help yourself." I add three spoonfuls of sugar to Grandma's current tea concoction.

"Sugar will do you in, Gabby," Mrs. Mott teases.

"I'll run an extra mile to burn it off," I tease back,

117

taking my usual seat at the table.

"So, how was your day?" Grandma leads.

"Crappy." I scowl. "Thanks a lot for sending Seth Jennings to me." I try to sound sarcastic, but it comes out more earnest.

"You know you want to help them. That poor man did not kill those people."

"I might be over my head here, though." I check the clock on the wall, it's nearly five now.

"You will manage, Gabriella, you always do," Grandma soothes.

I stand and turn on the TV to Lacey's channel. "You might feel differently after you see the news."

The women give me worried looks. "What did you do?" Grandma asks.

"Ran my mouth when I shouldn't have. Here it's coming on now, watch for yourself."

I turn up the volume and cringe as Lacey says "More developing news in the River Bend Bones case...."

I can barely stand to watch myself on the screen as Lacey pounces. The wind blows my curls and they fly around my head. The wild hair combined with the dark, tired smudges under my eyes really make me look like a crazy woman, or maybe a witch. I hardly recognize myself. When I stare directly into the camera and say "I'll prove it," I have to look away from the screen and bury my face in my hands. Maybe if I don't look at it, it didn't really happen.

"Oh, no," Mrs. Mott says, not unkindly.

"Gabriella, you didn't? On camera, to Lacey Aniston?

That woman hates you."

"I know, I know." I moan into my hands. "It gets worse."

"Worse than what we just saw?"

I raise my head. "I just talked to Diane Rawlings at the post office."

"Gabriella!" Grandma Dot scolds me.

"If I'm supposed to solve this case and help Seth and his dad out, I need information right?" I look at Mrs. Mott for reassurance.

She nods and says, "Diane Rawlings is a shrew."

"Yes she is. At first she talked to me because she didn't know any better. I did find out she and her daughter knew Steven was leaving them. But then they went to South Bend to stay with her mother, so she has an alibi. Plus, I know she didn't do it, I would have sensed it from Steven."

Grandma Dot shoots me a sharp look. I forgot she didn't know about last night's escapade with the bulldozer.

Grandma Dot squeezes my gloved hand. "Honey, you're not making sense. Why not start at the beginning," she says gently as if speaking to a child.

I tell them about how I found Steven last night. I watch Mrs. Mott's face closely at the really weird parts, hoping her expression doesn't turn to disgust or fear. It doesn't. If anything, she looks as concerned for me as Grandma Dot does. I could kiss both of them.

"All that sounds terrifying, dear," Mrs. Motts says as I finish. She reaches out for my other hand, my left one, but she doesn't notice. "You are so strong. I would die of fright."

"I nearly did die of fright," I joke, making light of the terror I felt.

The three of us sit quietly, holding hands. The acceptance soothes my raw nerves.

Two cars crunch across the gravel of the beauty shop parking lot, interrupting our quiet moment.

"That will be Seth Jennings and his brother Nicholas. I hope it's okay I asked them to meet me here so we could talk. I figured if anyone had information from back then, it would be you. And you, Mrs. Mott, an extra bonus. If you want to stick around and help out, that is."

"Of course, I'd love to! I haven't had this much excitement since I don't know when."

We watch the brothers as they cross the parking lot to the beauty shop door.

"The one in the suit doesn't look too happy," Mrs. Mott says.

"Must be Nicholas, Seth's older brother. He's also Patrick's attorney."

"Good heavens," Grandma Dot says to the ceiling as she crosses the kitchen to the sliding doors to the beauty shop to let the men in. "An attorney. This just gets better and better," she mumbles on her way out.

# Chapter 14

## GABBY

Grandma Dot dons her gracious hostess voice and ushers the brothers into the kitchen. "We're sitting in here. Would you boys like some tea?"

Seth readily agrees, Nicholas gives her a curt nod. Jet barks at the strangers.

"Nicholas, I haven't seen you since you went off to college," Grandma goes on.

Nicholas doesn't answer. From my seat across the room, I can feel his animosity towards us. No doubt he's used to fancy office meetings and conference rooms full of suits, not two old ladies and a paranormal chick sipping tea with a yapping dog jumping around. I take an instant dislike to the man. He's being rude to Grandma Dot in her own kitchen. I don't care if he likes me or not, but no one is rude to Grandma.

I glare at the man. He nervously straightens his already impeccable tie and slaps on a fake smile.

"Right. It has been a long time. Thank you for letting us hold this meeting here Mrs. Fredricks."

"Only my banker calls me Mrs. Fredricks. You can call me Dot." Her tight look and the fact she didn't say Grandma, tells me her opinion of the man matches mine.

"I'm Mrs. Mott." She reaches out her hand to Seth who takes it warmly. "Come sit with us." Seth dutifully sits next to me at the table, Nicholas lurks in the doorway, then concedes to at least stand near the bar.

He carefully places his briefcase on the bar, as if he's afraid it will get dirty. He drops the fake smile.

"Let's be clear right from the beginning. I'm handling the case against our father. I don't see the need for involving any of you in this." Right to the point.

"Nicholas, don't be rude. I asked Gabby to help us." Seth placates his brother.

"We don't need your kind of help," Nicholas stares directly at me, trying to intimidate.

His attitude grates. "You came to me, Mr. Jennings."

"My brother did, against my wishes."

"Well, either way. The evidence is stacked heavily against your father. If you can live with an innocent man going to prison, that's your problem. I know he didn't do it."

"You don't *know* anything. That's my point. Nothing you say will hold up in court. Even if I believed you, it

122

doesn't change a thing."

"I saw your mother die, Mr. Jennings. I lived through her final moments of fear. I also saw Steven Rawlings die. You can believe me or not, but I know your father didn't do it. Do you?"

Nicholas jumps as if slapped. "Do I what?"

"Do you know he didn't do it?" I let my words sink in. "Or do you think he did kill them and that's why you're so angry?"

"I...," he stammers.

"Nicholas, you know Dad didn't do it! He's not a killer," Seth shouts across the room. "And Gabby said it wasn't him."

Doubt covers his face. If he doesn't believe, this partnership will never work.

"I've got an idea," I say, standing up. "I can prove to you I'm not a fake."

"How?" Nicholas takes an involuntary step away from me. It's eerily like the step Dustin took.

I take off my left glove, and Nicholas watches with trepidation. "Think of something. Something meaningful, that you have strong feelings for."

"Why?"

"I will touch your hand and tell you what you are thinking about." I've never done this before, used my powers on purpose to prove them. I force confidence into my voice and say my usual silent prayer, "Lord, let me see what I need to see."

"Okay." I'm surprised he's agreed to my test. Most likely he expects me to fail.

"Do you have the image in your head?"

"Yes."

"Give me your hand." He holds it out, uncertain.

His hands are soft from pushing papers, softer than mine. I close my eyes. For a moment, I sense nothing and panic. This has to work.

Then a small yellow car shimmers into focus.

"A VW bug. The old style kind. It was your first car."

I open my eyes. Nicholas pulls his hand away as if burned. I look at the others. They stare wide-eyed. Even Grandma Dot. She's always believed, but never seen me do it like this before.

"How did you?" Nicholas looks more scared than impressed. "You knew about the car somehow."

"I told you to pick something. How would I know what you were going to pick. We've never even met."

"Seth told you. You two set this up." Nicholas grasps at straws and knows it.

"Pick something else. I'll do it again." I'm feeling good now, strong. He's lost the smug "I'm better than you" attitude.

"Do it again, Gabriella," Grandma Dot cheers me on.

"Either you believe me now, or let me do it again until you do," I challenge.

"Fine." Nicholas shoves his hand back to me.

"Think of something important to you."

"I am," he snaps.

I'm all warmed up and the vision focuses instantly.

"You cheated," I say, annoyed.

"Just because you can't guess it, I cheated?"

"I said pick something important to you. Either you *really* like file folders, or you purposely chose something with no meaning to you."

Nicholas falls heavily onto the kitchen bar stool.

He looks at his hand in disbelief. The others are silent, their jaws hanging open.

"Wow," Seth whispers.

"Yeah, wow," Mrs. Mott whispers too.

Grandma Dot just beams with pride. "Now that's out of the way, can we get on with the investigation?" she asks.

I slide my glove back on and put my other hand on Nicholas's shoulder, he doesn't flinch away. "When I say your father did not kill your mother or Steven, you can trust me."

The hopeful little boy look Seth gave me earlier appears on Nicholas's face now. "All these years, I always thought-," he says.

"Well, now you know."

"Come on Nicholas, let's figure out who did this to Mom," Seth says, scooting over to give his brother a seat at the table.

Nicholas takes the seat next to Seth. He pulls out a notepad and pen from his briefcase, all business.

I get my own pad and pen from the junk drawer and sit down too.

"The only way to clear Dad is to figure out the real killer," Nicholas starts. "What do we know so far?"

"It's someone both of them knew," I offer. "And it's not Diane, Steven's wife. I already talked to her and she was in South Bend that night."

Nicholas and Seth both look at me, surprised at my initiative. Seth shoots his brother an 'I told you so' look.

"Does anyone come to mind to you boys?" Grandma Dot asks. "Did you guys even know Steven Rawlings?"

"We were only eight and ten at the time. I really don't remember much," Seth says. "We heard a lot about him after they left, but I don't remember knowing him before."

"Me either. We did go to a lot of parties with other families. I remember playing with other kids, but not the adults," Nicholas pipes in.

We sit quietly, thinking. Jet scratches at my leg and I pull him into my lap.

"Grandma, you said there was a lot of talk then about the affair. Do you remember how they met or anything helpful?" Grandma squishes her face, thinking.

"There were all kinds of rumors, but nothing concrete. I feel like they ran in the same circles, went to the same barbeques and things, you know. Maybe that's how they met. Do you remember, Patty?"

Mrs. Mott looks out the window, thinking. "Gosh, there's been a lot of scandals since then. Wasn't Karen about Emily's age?"

"I think Emily was a few years younger, but they might have run in some of the same circles." Grandma looks at me. "Maybe your mom will remember something. Your parents went to a lot of those kinds of things too. You know, young families getting together. You might have been at some of the same parties."

Grandma lights up at the idea.

"I was only five then," I point out.

"Oh, that probably won't help, then," Grandma says, defeated a little.

"Can't we talk to your mom and ask her?" Seth points out.

The two older women and I share a look. "She's unavailable," I say simply. Nicholas just barely trusts me as it is. I can't imagine he'll be too pleased to know my mother's in prison for murder.

"So we've got nothing," Nicholas says.

"It had to be someone both of them trusted, and who also didn't like your dad. The bodies were buried on his farm. The killer could be framing him for the murders. Which he is, just twenty years later," I say. "So who had access to your farm? The bodies were way back on the tree line far from your house. I saw both victims get into a car with someone. How did the killer get them to the field?"

"I know the answer!" Mrs. Mott pipes in, excited to help.

We all look at her expectantly.

"The neighborhood next door now, the one where Dustin lives, was under construction then. Just some gravel drives and a few lots started up front. I remember because Dale and I bought one of the first houses in that neighborhood and it was the same time when Karen ran off." Mrs. Mott's pale purple poof bobs in her excitement. "The killer could have easily driven to the back of the neighborhood and dragged the bodies into the field from

127

there. No one would have seen a thing at night," she finishes with a self-satisfied smile.

I think about how the information matches my visions. "It fits," I state. "So the killer tricks them into a car, stabs them and drags them to the field. Knives are easy to come by, so no real lead there. I do wonder what order they were killed in. The car would have been bloody after the first murder. Did the second victim not see the blood in the car? Did the killer clean up between stabbings? Whoever was killed second would not get into a car with blood all inside it."

I stop talking because I feel Nicholas and Seth staring at me, their faces pale. "Gabriella, stop," Grandma Dot chastises. Too late, I realize I've been talking so blasé about blood and stabbing and dragging, forgetting it's their mother I am talking about.

"I'm sorry," I hurry to say. "That was insensitive."

"It's okay. We're going to hear a lot worse from the police and especially in court if this goes to trial," Nicholas says.

"We will figure this out. I will talk to my mother on Sunday and ask her what she remembers."

The day fades into full dark outside the window and fatigue climbs inside me suddenly. My little stunt with Nicholas along with my late night findings yesterday have sapped my energy. Jet lets out a little yelp from my lap, sensing my change in mood.

Grandma senses it too. "Well, boys, this has been enough for tonight." Grandma picks up the tea cups and takes them to the sink, a none too subtle hint.

The brothers stand and gather their things as well. "Please keep me informed if you find out anything," Seth says to me.

"I will, you do the same. We have to work together." I look pointedly at his brother, still not completely trusting him.

"Thank you, Gabby." Seth smiles, open and friendly. "You're really amazing."

I don't know what to do with the kind words. No one has ever called me amazing before, at least not about my gift. I hold the compliment close, like a tiny precious stone.

# Chapter 15

She's on the news again. Defiant and sure.

She steals the attention that should be mine.

I yearn to smash that lovely face. I need to cut her, to stop her.

I need to show her my power.

I shake with fury. The room closes in. I pace the short space, my steps carry me too fast to the other side. The cage constricts.

I caress my favorite blade. The glint of the steel entices, begs for blood.

I expose my thigh in the dingy light of the kitchen. Scars run at intersecting angles along my skin. Previous losses to the urge raised in lumpy testament.

The blade slides into my thigh in a practiced move. Freshly sharpened, the metal opens the skin easily. Deep red seeps from the cut, drips in beautiful splashes of color. Deep pain feeds my need, centers me.

I smear the blood, revel in the sticky warmth. I lick it

from my fingers, moaning at the familiar salty taste.

My blood can't compare to theirs. Memories of the knife sliding into his chest swamp me. I didn't do it for the blood, not that first time. The first plunge was over too quickly. The hot spurt splashed my face, dripped down my chin. The surge of ecstasy surprised me, spurred me on. I took my time after that. Sliced more carefully, savoring the moment. Too soon, he was gone.

I hungered.

I enjoyed the woman more. Timed it better, made it last.

Too soon, she was gone too.

The thirst raged.

The others couldn't quench it.

Now she threatens to destroy it all.

I must destroy her first.

I wipe my own blood from the blade. Soon hers will replace it. I know how to make it last now.

# Chapter 16

## GABBY

I half expect a mob with pitchforks to be waiting when I get home. My empty yard stretches under the overhanging trees, not a pitchfork in sight. As I climb out of my car, Preston comes out his door, the timing so perfect, I assume he was watching and waiting for me.

"Hey, Preston," I call as he approaches.

"So, how was your day?" he chuckles.

"I'm guessing you saw the news earlier. Lord, what a mess. I looked like the crazy person Lacey makes me out to be."

"I thought you looked cute." His smile is disarming, even in the moonlight.

"Why are you so nice to me?" I ask, kindly, suddenly

curious.

"Why shouldn't I be?" His tone is light, but I sense a tension.

"I don't know. Most people aren't." I think about Nicholas earlier. "Most people think I'm a fake. You don't seem to care about any of that."

"I do care. But I also understand it."

I cock my head in question.

"My grandmother had your gift too. Well, not exactly like yours, but she had powers too. She called it the shine."

"Like in the Stephen King book?"

"I guess so, I've never read it and I doubt she has either. People called her a fake, too. She didn't let it bother her. Her gift was part of who she was, but she was a lot of other things too. I guess that's why I like you. Your power is just part of you, it doesn't define you."

"That's some deep stuff," I say, trying to lighten the mood.

"I didn't mean it that way. So seriously, how was your day?"

"Considering I ticked off a few people, made a fool of myself on TV and got hired to solve an impossible crime, not too bad," I chuckle. "How was yours?"

"I sold three cars today, so pretty good."

"Sounds pretty good." This light, pointless conversation feels lovely after all the heavy stuff today. Not for the first time, I'm glad Preston moved in next door.

A stain on my garage door catches my attention.

Something yellow and sticky glints in the moonlight. I move closer to inspect it, my heart sinking. It's the remains of egg yolk, I've seen it enough times to recognize it. The driveway is wet and most of the egg is washed away. I give Preston a questioning look.

"It was there when I got home. I tried to wash it all off before you saw it, but I must have missed some."

A mix of shame at being egged and gratitude he cleaned up the mess overwhelms my already over-tired emotions.

"Thank you," I say simply, hoping my tone conveys the depth of my feelings.

"I was hoping you wouldn't find out about it."

We stand quietly in the dark, both staring at the small yellow smudge of hate on my garage door.

"Are we still on for the Corn Maze on Friday?" Preston changes the subject.

"As long as you bring your egg repellent," I quip, trying to be funny. It's a lame joke, but Preston goes along with it.

"I just bought two cans." We laugh softly together, then the mood shifts.

I don't need to be psychic to sense it. Preston wants to kiss me.

I almost let him, even lean a little closer to him. At the last moment, I pull away, uncertain.

To his credit, he plays it off well, just turns his eyes away.

To dampen my rejection, I say, "I'll see you Friday." It wasn't really a rejection, more like a postponement. I don't get involved with men easily. Exhausted from the day, I'm not ready to make that kind of decision.

I pat him on the shoulder awkwardly and hurry inside.

"Stupid, stupid, stupid," I say to Chester, and lock the door behind me.


The mist and shadows of the nightmare shift around me. Icy wind blasts my face, tosses my hair, but does nothing to dispel the mist.

"Gaaaabriiieeeelllaa." A woman's voice calls my name, drawing it out in an eerie sing song.

Spinning around, I only see mist and shadows.

"Gaaabriiieeelllaa." My name again, taunting, but in a man's voice.

I spin around and around, the wind stinging my face.

"Gabby!" The woman screams, right behind me.

I spin again.

The skeleton of Karen Jennings forms out of the mist. She raises her bony hand, reaches to touch me. The hand crumbles, the bones falling to the ground.

"I want it back, Gabby." The skeleton Karen hisses. "You stole me."

My feet stumble away from the horrible skeleton, catch in the dirt clods. Bony arms catch me before I fall.

"Careful, Gabby. You don't want to get hurt." It's Steven's skeleton. He places me carefully on my feet again.

Karen and Steven stand together, her non-shattered hand in his. The fog swirls through their bones, travels into their rib cages and pours out again.

Terror forces me to run. The line of yellow crime tape catches me.

The tape wraps around me, my struggles making it worse. The tape slithers around my body, a python crushing its victim.

The plastic slides around my neck, tightens.

I claw at the tape, desperate to breathe.

The skeletons have left me alone in the fog.


A weight presses on my chest as I wake from the nightmare. In a panic, I push the weight away. Chester howls as he flies across the room.

Consciousness catches up to me. "Sorry, Chester. I thought someone was trying to kill me."

I shake in my bed, blood pounding in my ears as the fear fades. I flip on my lamp to send the shadows away. A check of my phone shows I've only been asleep for an hour or so, it's not even midnight yet.

"Come here, Chester." I try to coax my cat back into bed with me, not wanting to be alone.

He gives me a haughty look and turns away. I don't blame him, I did toss him across the room.

Sleep, which I so badly need, eludes now. After a while, I give up and head to the kitchen for a glass of tea.

The lamp light from my room bounces down the short hall onto the curtains in my front room. My shadow towers in front of me, slides across the curtains, looks like a person. I jump back in fear, my nerves raw from the nightmare. My heart pounds again, adrenaline rushes in my blood.

It's just my shadow.

"Crap on a cracker," I mutter, laughing at my mistake. "Jumping at shadows."

I lean against the wall, catching my breath. Outside the living room windows, a car drives by slowly.

The headlights slide across the sheer curtains, illuminating the shape of a man.

This isn't my shadow. It's reflected from the lights outside, against the front window.

The car passes by and the front curtains turn dark again.

My blood sings with fear. I push against the wall, wanting to hide.

"Maybe I'm just imagining things," I console myself.

My feet drag slow steps to the front window, ready to run. The sheer fabric flutters gently from the heat register in the floor, the soft fabric a sharp contrast to the hard fear inside me.

Feeling exposed, I put my body against the front wall, some protection against whoever is outside.

My hand shakes as I slide back the thin curtain.

A few inches away from the glass, a hideous clown mask looks back at me. The oversized red mouth droops in a horrible frown, contrasting sharply with the white face. Grotesque blue paint surrounds the eyes holes. The man's real eyes glint behind the mask.

I drop the curtain back in place, duck against the wall.

And scream.

Outside the glass, the man laughs.

Fear freezes me against the wall. Rivulets of sweat drip

down my sides and my breath comes in ragged gasps.

The front door handle rattles.

A quick check verifies I locked the door earlier. The chain rattles as the man tries to get in.

He kicks the door and my body jumps into action.

I sprint to the kitchen, check the lock on the door to the garage.

"Go away! I have a knife!" I yell, taking a knife from a drawer. It's small, but sharp, the only protection I have.

"So do I, Gabby!" the man shouts back, the evil in his voice chilling. "Open the door and let me show it to you."

He slides the knife down the door making a sick scratching sound.

I feel trapped and exposed in the kitchen. I need to call for help.

I have to cross close to the front door to get to my room and my phone. Keeping my knife in front of me, I slide along the wall. I knock a picture off its nail. It crashes on my head and shatters at my feet.

The man outside laughs at my startled scream.

"Did you break something? Let me in and I can help you clean it up."

"I'm calling the cops!" I yell in reply.

I step over the broken glass and run for my phone.

He kicks at the door again, desperate to get to me.

I dial 9-1-1 and pray the wooden door will hold until help arrives.

The operator answers.

"This is Gabby McAllister. Someone's breaking into my house."

"Address please."

I give it to her.

"Did you say Gabby McAllister? Do you want me to send your brother?"

"Send whoever's closest! A masked man is beating down my door and says he has a knife. Just do your damn job!"

"Yes, ma'am. Someone is en route right now. Please stay on the line."

The beating on the front door stops, the quiet unnerving.

I peek down the hall. The closed front door stands silent in the shadows.

"He's stopped beating on the door," I tell the operator. "I think he's gone."

"Yes, ma'am," the operator replies. I don't like her sullen tone.

"Look, I'm sorry I cussed at you. I'm just scared."

"I understand, Gabby. This is Regina Hopkins, by the way."

The name sounds only vaguely familiar, but I fake it. "Oh, hi, Regina." I focus on the ridiculous conversation as I check my bedroom windows. No one outside, windows locked. "How are you?"

"Bobby and I are good. Married five years now," Regina, whoever she is, goes on.

I have no idea who Bobby is and I don't care. "That's nice," I say absently, checking the hall again.

In the distance, I hear the sirens approaching.

"I hear them coming now, Regina." Feeling braver, I

take a few steps down the hall.

"Good, stay on the line until they arrive. Would you like me to call your brother now?"

"No, that's not necessary. Can you call Detective Hartley? Or I can call him, I guess."

Regina takes a long moment to answer. "Yes, ma'am, I will inform Detective Hartley."

I notice she called me ma'am again, not Gabby.

A knock at the front door makes me jump. The sirens are still approaching, so it's not the police.

"Someone's knocking," I whisper to Regina, adrenaline pumping again.

"Gabby? It's Preston. Are you okay?" A loud knock again. "Gabby?"

"It's my neighbor. Thanks for your help, Regina." I hang up the phone before she can answer.

I slide the chain off and unlock the door.

Preston stands on my step, he's wearing pajama pants and sleep tousled hair.

The police car pulls in and skids to a stop.

"Police! Put your hands up!"

Preston looks at me in shock, and we both put our hands up. Always better to listen to the cops and explain later.

"This isn't the intruder," I tell the responding officer. "This is my neighbor."

We keep our hands up anyway until the officer approaches us.

"Are you the one who called in?" he asks me. I don't recognize the man.

I nod.

"And what are you doing here?" he asks Preston.

"I heard screaming, and came to check if she was okay." Preston looks at me with concern, his hands still in the air.

"The intruder is gone?" the policeman asks.

"I guess so. He was beating on the door, trying to get in. Then he stopped."

The policeman gives me an odd look. "You two can put your hands down now."

We nervously drop our hands.

"You're the woman I saw on the news, aren't you?" the officer asks. His tone leaves no doubt about what he thinks of me.

"Yes," I concede grudgingly.

"So some intruder beat on your door and then mysteriously disappeared?" the sarcasm drips off his words.

"Look, I heard her screaming. If she says someone was here, then they were," Preston jumps to my defense.

"And what did this *intruder* look like?"

"He had on a hooded jacket or coat of some kind, and he wore a clown mask. Nearly scared me to death. I hate clowns." I rub my bare arms against a sudden shiver.

"A clown mask, right."

I've had it with this man's attitude.

"Look, I don't know what your problem is. Do you treat all victims like you don't believe them?"

"Only ones that waste police time. First you go on TV and vow to set free a man who murdered two people.

142

Now you call in with an intruder story. I don't know what *your problem* is."

"*My problem* is some crazy person with a knife tried to break into my house wearing a clown mask and you're doing nothing about it!" I'm huffing in anger now. "Just wait until I tell my brother," I threaten. The words surprise me. I haven't used that ploy since we were kids.

"Your brother?" The obvious look of confusion makes me laugh.

"I'm Gabby McAllister, does the name Detective Dustin McAllister ring a bell?" His face goes pale.

My cell phone rings and I check the number.

"Or how about Detective Lucas Hartley? Ever hear of him? Here you want to talk to him and tell him how you're treating us?" I answer the phone. "Hi, Lucas. You want to set this officer," I pause looking at him for clarification.

"Brinkstone," he supplies.

"Want to set Officer Brinkstone straight? He's not taking this threat seriously." I hold my phone out to Officer Brinkstone. "Here, he wants to talk to you."

# Chapter 17

## LUCAS

My king size bed stretches empty around me. Weariness sinks bone deep. I don't remember the last time I slept.

My sheets hold a faint smell of old sweat. My ex-wife, Vivian, kept the house clean and neat. But she is far away in Indianapolis now with Olivia. They've been gone for over a year, but laundering the sheets has not been a priority. I miss the clean house and Olivia.

I make a mental note to change the sheets tomorrow, bury my face in the pillow and fade away.

My well deserved rest is short lived.

My phone rings, the special ringtone telling me it's dispatch. A shot of adrenaline wakes me up. I'm not on call tonight, dispatch shouldn't be calling me.

"Detective Hartley? This is Regina in dispatch."

"Hartley here." I rub my face, brace for what's coming next.

"Gabby McAllister called to report an intruder."

My previous exhaustion disappears.

"Is she okay?"

"She's fine." I don't like Regina's tone. "She is requesting you personally." Regina makes the statement sound like a question.

"I'll take care of it."

"I'm sure you will. I offered to call Detective McAllister, but she only wanted you." Regina sounds smug now. Her job requires a certain level of confidentiality, but she loves to gossip.

"Regina, you're on the job right now," I warn her. I'm not her supervisor, but I don't need her reading too much into the situation.

"Yes, sir." I don't miss the sarcasm. "Do you need the address?"

"I know where it is."

"Of course you do." I expect by tomorrow, the whole department will be buzzing that Gabby and I are an item. That could be bad, considering her stunt on the news today and her obvious role in the murder case.

I dial Gabby's number, and she picks up on the first ring. I expected her to be frightened, maybe even tearful. Instead she's angry. Gabby always keeps me guessing.

She puts Officer Brinkstone on the phone. Brinkstone is new to our department, and I don't know him well.

"Brinkstone, Detective Hartley here."

"Sir."

"Do you want to tell me why the victim is so upset?"

"This woman is wasting our time. There's no one here. She probably made the whole thing up, trying to get attention. You know who she is, obviously."

"I do know who she is, and she doesn't make up false claims about intruders." I slide on jeans as I talk, trying to keep my calm. I'm tired and grouchy, in no mood for dealing with a rookie who can't be professional.

"Brinkstone, are you wearing a badge right now?"

"Of course." The young officer sounds weary.

"Then right now, you are an officer. Protect and serve. Sound familiar? You leave your personal feelings behind when you put on that badge. If Gabby says someone threatened her, then you act on it. Do you understand?" I try to keep the anger at bay, but fail.

Someone tried to hurt Gabby. The thought pushes control out of my reach.

"Yes, sir," Brinkstone says, sounding like a chastised child.

"I will be there in a few minutes. In the meantime, you *serve* Gabby and *protect* her. Got it?"


It doesn't take long to get anywhere in River Bend. Soon I pull my cruiser in front of Gabby's house. Brinkstone is still here, standing several feet away, looking uncomfortable and angry. A man I don't recognize stands next to Gabby on her front step, helping her on with a jacket.

147

An unfamiliar surge of emotion surprises me. I focus on Gabby. Her curls blow in the breeze, her face seems pale in the light of the front stoop. She wraps the jacket tighter around her, crosses her arms against her chest. She looks vulnerable and strong at the same time.

Across the street, a curtain moves as a neighbor peeks out. I scan both directions down the street, into the neighboring yards. No one else is around. No one has come out to see if Gabby is okay, except the strange man near her. The presence of police vehicles late at night normally pulls a few nosy neighbors out. The lack of interest, especially in this neighborhood which rarely draws a police presence, annoys me. It's like no one cares.

I check my Ruger 9mm in its holster at my hip, the familiar movements soothing. The neighbors might not care what happens to her, but I do.

Gabby meets my eyes as I approach. She gives a little nod, as if to tell me she is okay.

"Brinkstone!" I snap at the rookie. To his credit, he squares his shoulders and faces me straight on. "Did you get what you needed for your report?"

A fast rub of his hand across his over-short crew cut shows his nervousness. "Yes, sir."

"So you noted the kick marks on the door? And the fresh scratches in the wood?"

Brinkstone's shoulders sag, and he takes out his notebook.

"I didn't think so. How about the way these bushes are crushed here by the window?"

Brinkstone scribbles.

I shine my flashlight on the soft dirt between the bushes and the window. "Or these footprints here? Does this look like she made this up?"

Brinkstone has the good sense to look sheepish. On another night, I might take pity on the rookie, but not tonight.

He scribbles some more. "Got it, sir."

"I'll take it from here," I say to the young officer.

He's only too happy to leave.

I turn my attention to Gabby and the strange man.

"Lucas, thank you for coming." Relief evident in her voice. I silently rail at Brinkstone again. She should have felt relief from his presence, but the man's a disgrace to the badge.

"And who is this?" I ask of the stranger standing next to her, my tone rougher than necessary.

"This is my neighbor, Preston. He heard me screaming and came to see if I was okay."

"Preston, I'm Detective Hartley, a friend of Gabby's and her brother's partner." I reach out my hand to shake his. I'm far enough away, Preston has to step down from the stoop and away from Gabby to shake it. He takes the bait, and shakes my hand. I squeeze harder than necessary, just to gauge his reaction. He squeezes back, looks me in the eye. He's a few inches shorter than I am, and has to look up slightly. We finally release hands.

"Thank you for checking on Gabby. I can take it from here." I use my best police voice. The man seems nice enough, but I really want him to leave.

Preston looks at Gabby. "I'd rather stay."

"I'm okay now, Preston, really. Thank you for checking on me. I was so scared." The quiver in her voice belies her "everything's fine" attitude.

Preston hesitates. I place my hand on my pistol at my hip, make it seem like an unconscious gesture.

Preston gets the hint.

"If you're sure you're okay," he says. "We're still on for Friday, right?"

Gabby gives him a bright smile. "Of course, looking forward to it."

The man sends a look at me over his shoulder, then walks away.

I turn my attention to Gabby. "Busy day?" I ask, trying to lighten the mood.

She laughs, the sweet sound tempered by nerves. "You don't know the half of it."

"I know enough."

She looks down sheepishly. "You and Dustin are angry with me, but Patrick Jennings' son came to me and asked me for help. What was I supposed to do?"

"You're supposed to stay out of it. We're talking about murder, Gabby. You could get hurt."

"But Patrick is innocent. You know that. Besides, what could happen?"

I spread my arms wide. "What happened here tonight, for starters."

She doesn't have an answer to that, looks past me across the yard, wraps her arms tighter across her chest.

"Let's start at the beginning. What did happen here

tonight?"

"Can we go inside first?"

We settle at the kitchen table, glasses of sweet tea in our hands. I recognize the recipe from the kind Grandma Dot serves.

"After I left the nursing home, I went to Grandma Dot's to meet with Seth and Nicholas Jennings." Gabby looks at me, expecting a comment. I don't say anything, just wait for her to go on.

"Then I came home. Someone egged my garage, but Preston had already cleaned it off. Stuff like that happens a lot, so I didn't think too much about it."

She tries to shrug it off, but I can tell by the set of her shoulders it bothers her.

"I went to bed and later, I woke up." I sense there's more to that line than she is letting on, but I let her talk.

"I saw a shadow outside my window. I looked out, and there was a man in a hooded jacket and a clown mask."

She stares past me, focuses on the refrigerator.

"I hate clowns," her voice trembles.

"Then what happened?" I encourage gently.

"I checked the door to the garage, grabbed a knife, then went for my phone and called 9-1-1. He started kicking the door, trying to get in. He said he had a knife."

Gabby's hand trembles on the glass of tea. I reach out to soothe her. Her skin is soft and warm. She isn't wearing gloves. For the first time I touch her bare hand.

"I told the man the police were coming, and the banging on the door stopped. Then Preston was here."

"He showed up right after the banging stopped?"

151

Gabby gives me a sharp look. "He wasn't the man in the window."

"I didn't say he was, I'm just getting the facts straight. Do you have any idea who might want to harm you?"

"How many people live in this town?" she says sarcastically.

"Not everyone hates you, Gabby."

"Tell that to the punks who painted on my door the other day, or the ones who egged me tonight. Normally, it's just little things. No one has ever openly threatened me until now."

She stares at the fridge again, lost in her pain. It can't be easy being a target all the time.

"Then that officer acts like I'm the criminal. I'm so sick of everyone!" She jumps up from her chair and crosses to the kitchen sink. She splashes water on her face, and dries it on a hand towel, stares out the window. "Why did you have to involve me in this? My life was bad enough before, now everyone knows what I am and hates me for it."

Guilt stabs me. It is my fault she's involved. I move close behind her, so close I can smell the peaches of her shampoo. "Gabby, I'm so sorry. I never meant for this to get so out of hand."

She's close enough to touch, but I don't move.

Our faces are reflected in the kitchen window, our eyes meet in the reflection.

"I know you didn't. There's a reason I have this gift. If I can find justice for Karen and Steven and keep Patrick out of prison, then it's worth it."

"You're amazing, you know that?"

She lets out a huff of disbelief.

"Really. You're one of the strongest people I know. You were nearly attacked tonight and you're thinking about justice for others. Most people would be crying in their beds right now."

"Don't worry, I'll cry myself to sleep later." She turns from our reflections and smiles at me. It lights up her face, crinkles around her eyes. I can feel the heat of her body near mine. Confused, I take a step back.

"Speaking of sleep, do you want me to stay with you tonight?" Her eyes widen in surprise. "On the couch," I add quickly. "My cruiser's parked out front and with me here, you can get some rest."

"I'd like that." Her voice is low and quiet. "Thank you."

A short time later, Gabby has me tucked into blankets and pillows on her couch. The bedding smells sweet, with a hint of lavender. I set my holster on the coffee table, nearby as always.

She stands at the end of the hall, the light from her bedroom glows around her, softens the shadows in the living room. "Do you have everything you need?"

"I'm all set."

She hesitates in the hall, her face hidden by shadow.

"I'm glad you're here, Lucas."

"Me too, Gabby."

I sense she wants to say something else. Silently, she turns and walks down the hall. The light goes dim as she shuts her door.

I lay back on the couch, stare at the ceiling, getting familiar with the shadows and shapes of the room. The couch isn't nearly as comfortable as my king size bed at home.

There's no where I'd rather be right now.

# Chapter 18

## GABBY

With Lucas and his gun in the next room, I sleep soundly and wake surprisingly refreshed. The morning sunshine pours in my windows, chasing away the terror of last night. Quiet, rhythmic snoring from the couch fills me with both peace and a strange longing. Or maybe that's just the aftereffects from last night. Either way, I need coffee.

A quick peek in the living room shows Lucas curled on his side, wrapped in my favorite yellow blanket. His face, softened by sleep, looks younger. The crinkles around his eyes are loose, not sharp and calculating like when he is awake, taking in details, searching. His mouth hangs softly open, not grim and determined. The strange longing slips through my chest again, confusing me.

I spin on my heel, away from the sleeping man.

The sound of the coffee maker changes the pattern of his quiet snoring.

"Do you want coffee?" I call from the kitchen.

"Sounds good," he calls back, barely a note of drowsiness in his voice.

Lucas sits upright, the soft face of sleep replaced by the sharp watching eyes I'm more familiar with. His short hair is barely mussed, like he didn't move while he slept. I hand him the coffee cup and sit on the couch with him, the only other seat available in my small living room.

"Cream and lots of sugar, right?" I ask, unnerved by the intimacy of this early morning domestic situation.

Lucas must feel the awkwardness too. He won't meet my eyes, just focuses on his coffee.

I follow his lead and sip quietly.

I finally ask the question I refused to consider last night.

"Do you think the man at my window was the real killer trying to scare me off the case?"

Lucas shows no surprise at my question. Just sighs heavily and rubs at the heavy stubble on his chin.

"I don't know, Gabby. It definitely wasn't Patrick Jennings."

"And Patrick Jennings isn't the killer," I point out, an edge of irritation in my voice.

"All the clues point to him." He looks at me side-eyed. "They were found on his property. His wife was leaving with Steven. He's the only one with motive to kill them both."

"He didn't kill them." My voice is firm, sure. "I told you it wasn't him. There's a killer out there right now."

"All the more reason for you to stay out of it until we know for sure." Lucas suddenly slams his cup down on the coffee table. A small splash of brown spreads across the table. "Crap!" he mutters and hurries to the kitchen for a rag.

His strong reaction surprises me. "Why are you so angry this morning?"

"Why do you think, Gabby? You're putting yourself in danger and don't even care." He grumbles as he cleans up the splash, knocking the cup over in his agitation. More coffee spreads across the table.

I hurry to the kitchen for paper towels.

We clean up the mess together in silence, his anger and fear radiating off of him.

I place my hand on his upper arm. "Lucas, talk to me." It's my left hand, and I don't have a glove on. He looks pointedly at my hand, and I expect him to pull away in horror. He places his own hand on top of mine and gives a small squeeze. The tiny motion nearly drowns me.

"I can't keep you safe if you keep putting yourself in danger," he says quietly.

"It's not your job to keep me safe." A mixture of defensiveness and hope in my words.

"I'm a police officer. It is my job."

His words hit like a punch, and I snatch my hand away. The hope dissolves, only defensiveness left. "So sorry, to be a burden, Detective Hartley," I snap.

"Gabby-," he tries.

"Thank you for protecting me last night. Above and beyond the call of duty, and all that." I grab the spilled cup and rags and storm into the kitchen.

"That's not what I meant, and you know it," he calls after me.

"I don't know anything! That's the point." Vaguely, I realize I'm not making sense, but emotion courses through me, and words tumble from my mouth. "Just go. I can take care of myself. I won't bother you again."

"Gabby, seriously," he pleads.

I slam the wet paper towels into the trash. Disappointment washes over me. I've always thought Lucas was different, liked me in some small way. How did we go from the sweet moment when he actually touched my hand on purpose to this?

"Just go!" I yell, startling us both.

We lock eyes across the kitchen. Confusion in his, hurt anger in mine. Both our chests heave, the sound of our breathing mixing with the sputtering of my coffee maker. The moment stretches. I open my mouth to apologize, when his phone rings.

He glances at the screen. "It's Dustin. I have to take this. It might be important." His eyes plead for me to understand.

I want to say "this is important, too," but I snap my mouth shut against the words.

"Hartley," he answers the phone. "I know. I'm with her now. Ok, be right there." He stabs the button to hang up on my brother.

"I have to go." I convince myself the hurt and longing I hear in his voice is just my imagination.

"Yes, you do. I notice he called you and not me." I turn my back on him and rinse out our coffee cups, unwilling to let him see my pain.

I sense him hesitate at the door, watching me.

I refuse to turn around.

The door closes behind him with a thunk echoing through my small home. Tears come, the moment his car pulls away. I have crushed something precious. This morning had so much promise, and then spun out of control. Lucas has been a good friend to me, has stood by me when most people don't. I repaid him by throwing a fit because I didn't like the way he phrased something.

"You stupid girl!" I shout at myself. "When will you learn to trust people?"

The coffee maker sputters in response.


The pounding of the music in my earbuds matches the pounding of my feet on the gravel jogging path at the park. I need to run today. I'm going to be late to work, but I don't care. With everything going on and now the fight with Lucas, I deserve an hour to myself. Herbert will just have to deal with it.

I haven't run since the morning Dustin called me about finding Karen. That feels like weeks ago to my mind and to my legs. I tire more quickly than usual. The covered bridge looms ahead and I turn to the refuge it offers. The wooden planks shake as I thump across them. Half-way across, I stop to catch my breath.

The river rolls away below me as I lean over the dusty, splintered sides of the bridge. Weak light filters through the roof, dapples of beauty surrounding me. I pull out my earbuds and listen to the water flowing below, the wind whipping through the bridge. This bridge is a tourist attraction of sorts in River Bend, but the cold, windy weather has driven everyone away.

I have the bridge to myself.

I can't get Karen out of my mind. She's been dead for years, but she's trying to tell me something. Last night's dream echoes through my memory, niggles at my mind. Karen saying "You stole me," and her hand disintegrating replays on a loop.

The wind picks up, sharp and biting. It fits my mood. My usual running jacket is no match for the October weather. My tattoo begins to burn and I try to rub it away. There's no one around, no one that needs me.

I'm alone in the cold.

I unzip my pockets, shove my hands inside to keep warm.

Something hard in my pocket nearly burns me and I pull my hand away with a startled squeal. Confused, I put my hand back in my pocket and take out the object.

Karen's finger bone lays on my gloved palm.

My tattoo tingles, and my mind swims.

I slide off my left glove and clasp the bone in my fist.

The vision of Karen standing next to me hits so hard, so clear, my legs collapse beneath me and I lean against the wooden walls of the bridge.

*"Protect my boys, Gabby. Protect Patrick. They deserve so much more than I gave them by leaving."*

*Karen looks over her shoulder, listening to someone I can't see.*

*"Look after Rachel, too. We were stolen from our children, can't protect them now. They grew up without us, that was never our plan. You have to protect them now. You are all we have Gabby."*

I struggle to speak, to ask questions. My voice finally works and I scream "Who did it?!" But Karen is gone.

I'm alone on the bridge.

Pain and loss sear through me. I throw the bone across the bridge in terror. It rattles across the planks, rolls to a gap in the wood floor and nearly slips through. I lunge across the floor, landing hard on my knee. Ignoring the pain, I snatch the bone before it disappears forever. I shove the bone back in my pocket and back up against the wall again.

Huddling against the wooden wall, loss overwhelms me. Sobs tear my chest, hot tears slide from my tightly clenched eyes. I miss my own father. Torn away from me, replaced with this ability to see pain and fear. Karen's loss mixes with my own, an unbearable shredding pain. I wrap my arms around my knees, lower my head and give in to the misery as the cold wind whips through the bridge.

I cry for her death, for the pain left behind for her family to bear. I cry for Steven murdered and left in a field. Mostly, I cry for myself. Guilty, choking sobs of grief for the life I lost when my father was killed and my mother taken away. I cry for the shattered pieces of my life I can't seem to fit back together.

Something cold and wet touches my cheek, startling me out of my tears.

"JoJo, leave her alone," a woman says to a small black and white dog on a leash. Her presence startles me. Lost in agony, I didn't hear her steps on the planks.

I stare up at the woman, guiltily wiping at my tears. "Are you okay, dear?" Crinkles of concern etch her face.

"Yeah, I'm fine." I hastily climb to my feet, embarrassed to be caught in such a vulnerable state.

The woman looks me over closely, the way I imagine a mother would. "I'm sorry we intruded, but JoJo insisted on walking this way."

"That's okay. I was just-." I don't know how to finish the sentence.

"You don't need to explain. Sometimes all we can do is cry it out, you know." The woman stands patiently, waiting for me to get myself together. JoJo, the dog, sits at her heels, cocks his head at me in curiosity.

I quickly put my glove back on and try to think of a polite way to get out of the conversation.

"You're the psychic woman helping with that murder case, aren't you?" The woman sounds impressed, not angry, but I'm weary just the same.

"Uh, yeah." I dart my eyes to the end of the bridge, anxious to get away.

She stretches her hand and pats me on the shoulder. "God bless you for what you're doing." Her words surprise me more than the touch from a stranger. "There's no way Patrick Jennings killed his wife and her friend. Someone has to find out the truth."

"Do you know Patrick?" Thoughts of fleeing are gone. Finally, someone believes me.

"Known him for years, poor man. Thinking Karen walked away from him and the boys nearly broke his heart. And all this time, she had been murdered. She and the Rawlings man."

She has my full attention now. "Did you know Steven too?"

"I knew them both. I was a math teacher at the high school for 30 years, retired now. I've taught nearly everyone in this town, or their kids. River Bend was a much smaller town back when Karen and Steven disappeared. Everyone was talking about it. When they never contacted their families, both Patrick and Steven's wife tried to file missing person's reports, but the police weren't interested. Said they ran off and started a new life. I knew Karen would never just walk away from her boys, or Stephen from Rachel, for that matter. It never sat well with me."

I look at the woman, curious if I can trust her.

I choose to trust.

"I just talked to Karen, and Steven."

I drop the words on her, judge her reaction. Her eyes open wide, but she believes me. JoJo, the dog, yips quietly from his place by her heels. "You did?"

"Just now. Here. She asked me to protect their kids."

"Sounds like Karen," the woman shakes her head. "You have an amazing gift. I wish I could help like you are."

My earlier misery has morphed into excitement. "You have been a help. At least it's nice to know someone other than me knows Patrick is innocent."

"God bless you. It can't be easy doing what you do."

"No, it isn't."

"The police seem so eager to blame Patrick. You might be the only one who can save him."

The weight of the responsibility settles on my shoulders, dampens my mood.

"Don't worry, dear. You're a strong, smart woman. You will figure it out. You were right about the fire at the basketball game. You are right about this."

The infamous basketball game incident has come back to haunt me again.

"Don't look so startled," the woman says. "I was at that game. I'll never forget your face when you came running in yelling fire. You were so scared. And so brave."

"No one else thought I was brave, everyone hated me after that." I sound sullen and petty, even to myself.

"I heard directly from administration there really was a fire in the utility room. If it wasn't for you, the school could have burned down, or worse."

"But no one believed me."

"Doesn't mean you didn't save the day."

JoJo jumps against my legs. He'd been standing quietly while we talked, but is eager for attention now.

"See, JoJo believes in you."

I pet the little dog. "I'm glad you wanted to walk this

way today, JoJo."

"Maybe he has some of your powers," the woman suggests with a smile.

# Chapter 19

## DUSTIN

They try to hide it, but I catch the sideways glances and whispered comments. I don't have to be a detective to know everyone at the station is talking about my sister's stunt on the news yesterday.

A message from Regina in dispatch doesn't help my mood any.

"Your sister called about an intruder last night. She didn't want me to tell you, but asked for Detective Hartley instead. I just thought you should know."

Anger stabs me. The petty vandalism the other night bothered me enough, but an intruder? I rub the tension in my neck. I should call and check on her, but decide to call

Lucas first and get the story.

He's with her this morning.

Why does everything with her have to be so complicated?

Lucas looks ragged when he arrives at the station. He's wearing street clothes and badly needs a shower and shave. The set of his shoulders keeps me from mentioning it.

We settle into my office with coffee. The bitter taste lingers even with plenty of sugar and cream. Nothing like the mocha lattes I prefer. Lucas swallows his in quick gulps.

"Bad morning?" I ask, trying to lighten the heavy cloud he brought with him.

"Bad couple of days. Your sister's going to ruin me."

I sip my bitter coffee and wait for him to go on.

"Someone tried to break into her house last night," he finally says.

"I read the report. Some freak in a clown mask."

"She thinks it might be the killer coming after her."

This thought had already crossed my mind. We're pretty sure Jennings is guilty, but until we can make an arrest, nothing is certain.

"Is that why you stayed there last night?" I can't keep from asking.

Lucas eyes me suspiciously.

"It wasn't like that. She was pretty shook up, so I offered to sleep on the couch to keep watch."

I don't pursue that line of questioning. They're both adults, what they do is their business. Plus, she's my sister, and there's some things I don't want to know about.

"Do you think she's in danger?" I ask.

"She thinks she is, that's all that matters." There's an undercurrent to his words, and I get the feeling I'm being chastised.

I stare at the pale concrete blocks of my office wall, try to push away the guilt. Gabby asked for his help, not mine. "Maybe we should keep a closer eye on her, just in case. She won't like it."

"She's going to the corn maze tonight with some guy." Hartley drops the words.

"What guy?"

"Her neighbor. He was with her when I arrived last night."

I mull this information over. Gabby rarely dates, barely has friends, even. I don't know much about her private life, but Grandma Dot keeps me informed whether I ask or not.

"Let's check this guy out, just to be sure he's not the threat."

"Already planned to." Lucas watches me over his coffee cup, a smug expression on his face.

"I think Alexis and Walker would enjoy going to the corn maze, too," I add.

Lucas stands abruptly, slaps me on the shoulder. "Good man, McAllister."

# Chapter 20

## GABBY

After the intruder last night, my fight with Lucas, and the vision on the bridge this morning, I don't feel like going to work. Between explaining to Herbert why I need time off, or just going in, I choose work. I struggle through the day, try to focus on the customer's needs, but my mind keeps drifting to the murder. I wish Karen would just tell me who killed her and be done with it. I'd still have to prove it, but I'd have something to go on.

The hours drag by, but eventually the work day ends. I stretch my back and grab my coat, anxious to leave.

"Gabby, wait up." My friend Haley catches me at the front door. "Got any plans for the weekend?"

The normal question catches me off guard. Not for the

first time, I'm jealous of "regular" people and "regular" concerns. I haven't been "regular" for years. I like Haley, and for the moment I indulge myself.

"I have a date tonight." Her eyes flash wide.

"Ooh, nice. Where're you going?"

"The corn maze," I shrug.

Haley laughs. "That's so Indiana." We push out the doors into the parking lot. "What're you going to wear?" Haley is only two years younger than me, but right now I feel old.

"I haven't thought about it."

"I know you're busy with this investigation and being on the news and all, but it's okay to have some fun. Go buy a nice outfit. Always makes me feel better."

"Maybe," I shrug.

"Want me to come with you?" Her open expression invites, but I turn her down anyway.

"I'll be fine, but thanks."

"Call me if you change your mind. Enjoy your date!" Haley turns away with a wave.

I sit in my Charger in the parking lot, watching the other employees get in their cars and drive away to their various lives. A heavy, familiar loneliness settles on me. I suddenly wish I had taken Haley up on her offer to shop with me, even pick up my phone to call her. I don't want to look desperate, and put my phone away again. I do have my date with Preston tonight, but in my current mood, even that doesn't excite me.

"Well, get excited, kid. This is your life," I mutter to myself and drive to the store.

Once at the store, I don't feel like buying a new outfit. I have a few hours until Preston is picking me up, and I don't want to go to my empty house alone. Instead, I take my usual seat at the coffee shop in the superstore and people-watch. I'm not really paying attention, though, and when a woman with three small children approaches me, I jump.

"Gabby, are you okay?" the woman asks. Her face is vaguely familiar, but her voice I recognize instantly from my 9-1-1 call last night. "Did Detective Hartley take care of you?" Regina asks. I hear the tiny undercurrent of insinuation in her words, but I ignore it.

"Yes, he took care of it. Thank you. Sorry I was so rough with you. I was pretty freaked out."

"I can only imagine. How terrifying." Uncomfortable silence settles around us. I'm not good with small talk. Regina has two small children hanging on her and one in a stroller.

"Cute kids," I finally say to fill the space.

"They keep me busy." She absently ruffles the hair of the tallest child and gently rolls the stroller back and forth to keep the toddler quiet. She obviously has something on her mind and I wish she would get to it.

"Do you really think that man is innocent?" she finally asks.

"Yes, I do," I state simply.

She looks out across the store, deep in thought. "I remember when they left. Or were murdered, I guess."

"Did you know Karen and Steven?" She has my

173

interest now.

The toddler in the stroller starts to fuss. Regina rocks him a little faster, her mind still far away and an uncertain expression on her face.

"I didn't really know them, but my brother dated Rachel in high school."

Just then the little one in the stroller hollers and throws his toy. A pink stuffed pig drops on the floor of the coffee shop, rolls against my foot. I hand it back to the boy. He grabs it with a pudgy hand, but lets out another wail.

Her child's cry brings Regina back to the present. "Guess, he's tired of sitting still," Regina laughs nervously.

"Cute pig toy," I offer.

"He loves pigs. Has to have it with him at all times. We bought four identical ones just to be sure he always has one near."

"Good idea." I have no idea what else to say. I open my mouth to ask about her brother, but the toddler hollers again, cutting me off.

"I better get moving," Regina says. "Glad everything worked out okay for you last night." Regina hurries away with the stroller and the two other children in tow.

I almost expect my house to look different after last night's violation. Except for the knife marks on the front door, the small house looks the same. I'm the one who's changed. I look around the neighborhood and sit in my car. I feel vulnerable and anxious.

"Crap on a cracker, Gabby. Just go in." Frustrated

174

with my dramatics, I shove the car door open with a screech and strut with pretend confidence to my front door.

A hot shower and carefully applied makeup improves my mood and I find myself looking forward to my date with Preston. Wrapped in a towel, I scan my closet for something to wear. The usual collection of jeans, sweaters and long sleeve t-shirts stare back at me. I wish I had listened to Haley and bought something cute for tonight. My lack of social life shows in my wardrobe. I rarely have a need for anything other than basic comfort.

Doing the best I can with what's available, I settle on a black sweater, my tightest jeans and ankle boots. Preston has only seen me in my usual sloppy clothes and still likes me. I console myself he isn't expecting a beauty queen. Chester rubs against my leg and purrs. At least he likes the outfit.

Grandma Dot gave me special curl tamer oil, but I rarely use it. I feel indulgent tonight, and apply liberal amounts to my usual wild mass of hair. The oil smooths my curls into soft ringlets. I study myself in the mirror, and hardly recognize the reflection. Feeling inspired, I add silver dangling earrings.

The girl in the mirror smiles and raises her chin. "You clean up pretty good, kid." I meet my own eyes in the mirror, the corners crinkled from my genuine smile. "You can handle this," I tell myself, talking about more than the date. "You're stronger than you think. God's got your back. Just follow him and it will all work out." A surge of peaceful confidence pumps through me, straightening my back and pulling my shoulders straight.

A knock at the front door intrudes on the moment.

"Just a minute," I call out to Preston.

A quick glance back in the mirror, and I grab my mascara. A few extra swipes on my eyelashes and I feel ready for my date.

# Chapter 21

For twenty years, I've waited for her to come back to me. I wake everyday thinking today's the day she will realize what I mean to her. She'll see what I did for her and come back.

That witch on the news was harder to get to than I thought. Time to push forward with my plan.

Today's the day she'll realize that she can't live without me.

I know her schedule better than my own. How many hours have I spent watching her, following her? I have watched her whole life from afar. Glimpses through parted curtains. Conversations overheard. Longing filling every cell of my body.

I waited for the miracle. The moment she'd turn and see me, know it was me she had been waiting for as well.

That miracle didn't come.

I had to entertain myself with pale substitutes for her.

Practice my skills.

Taking her will be easy. I could have taken her at any of a thousand moments before.

Today she'll be mine.

She drops her kids off at their father's. That stupid man who had her in his grasp, but let her get away. I knew it wouldn't last. She belongs to me.

I don't follow her for the drop-off. I've seen the exchange before. I let myself into her house. I've done it before, even stole a key and made a copy. I feel closest to her walking through her space, touching her things, smelling her clothes.

I wait in her kitchen, sipping a soda from her fridge, slowly eating an apple from the bowl on the counter. The sound of my chewing mixes with the whir of the fridge.

The clock on her stove slowly ticks the minutes away.

Excitement jumps through me, the wait excruciating and sweet.

Her garage door rumbles up and I get into position just inside the door into the kitchen.

My breath comes harsh and ragged, I can barely contain myself.

The door opens beside me.

The waiting ends.

My arm slides around her neck and my knife pushes against her throat in one smooth motion. I've played this moment in my mind so many times, the reality of it shakes me.

"Hello, Rachel. I've missed you." I purr into her ear. "Have you missed me?"

Rachel whimpers in response. Her body trembles against mine. The smell of fear mixed with her perfume excites me. I want to cut her, but wait. There will be time for the blood later.

"Come now, you have nothing to say to me after all these years? You had plenty to say in high school."

Another whimper and she scratches at my arm around her neck. I ignore the sting and pull her tighter against my chest.

"Remember the nights we spent in the back seat of my car? You liked me plenty then. Couldn't get enough of me, as I recall." I push my hips against her.

She says my name in question. That word from her lips draws a groan from deep within me.

"Say my name again," I whisper close to her ear.

Nothing.

I push the tip of the knife into her skin, and she complies. She repeats my name three times, barely audible.

I fight to control my response.

"That's better."

I inhale deeply, holding the scent of her inside my lungs. The need almost wins.

I push it away. I've waited years for this. I won't ruin it now with haste.

"This is going to be simple. My car's parked out front. We're going to walk out like nothing is wrong. If you scream, or make any sudden movement, I will kill you. Do you understand?"

Rachel nods silently.

"And lock the door behind us. You don't want some crazy person breaking in."

Rachel moves stiffly, dragging her feet, but she complies.

"Good girl, Rachel," I soothe her once we're seated in my car. "We're going to have such a happy life together. We've missed so many years, but I know you're worth the wait."

Rachel looks at me, tears streaking her precious face. A strand of her lovely blond hair catches in the wetness. I brush it away, ignore her flinch at my touch.

"Why are you doing this?"

"So we can be together. Everything I've done is for you, Rachel."

She doesn't understand, but she will.

"Now, this is going to hurt, but just a little. I can't risk you getting away from me now."

The stun gun I've modified catches her by surprise. Her body convulses several times, then relaxes.

Her pulse flutters a moment, then steadies out. I kiss the spot on her silky neck, touch her skin with the tip of my tongue.

The most delicious candy.

Rachel stirs as I lay her gently on the bed I have ready for us in my spare bedroom. I quickly secure the cuff and chain on her ankle before she regains full consciousness.

Her eyes flutter open, her beautiful lashes blinking several times before she focuses on me. She scrambles across the bed, trying to get away. The chain rattles across the bed spread as she backs into the corner where the bed is pushed against the wall.

Her eyes are wide, like a frightened animal.

Her fear pains me, but I expect it. She will learn to love me again.

"Shh, you're safe now. I'm here," I coo at her, gently rubbing her leg to calm her. She pulls her leg away. "Do you like your room? I went to a lot of work to make it just right for you. It's only temporary, a place to keep you safe until you remember."

Rachel looks around the room, confused and curious.

"I painted the walls your favorite color, pale blue. This bedding matches the one on your bed at your house, see?"

Her eyes lock on the pictures hanging on the wall.

"Where did you get those?" she demands.

"Those are of your kids," I say simply.

"I know who they are," she snaps. "Where did you get them?"

"From your house. You had so many, I didn't think you'd miss them. But I wanted you to feel at home here. I even have some of your clothes in the closet."

"This will never be my home." Her eyes snap, but her lip quivers.

"We'll see about that, my love." I touch her face, sliding my fingers against her cheek. She pulls away, turns to the wall.

"You must be thirsty. Here drink this, you'll feel better."

She doesn't reach for the cup I hand her. "Don't be rude, Rachel. I've gone to a lot of trouble to make you feel welcome. Don't ruin it." I struggle to keep my voice steady and soothing. I look pointedly at the knife on the other side of the room. I know she can't reach it with the leg chain on. I prepared for that as well.

Rachel looks at the knife, then reaches for the cup.

"Good girl, now drink it all." Her lips on the cup and her swallowing motions drive me to the edge. "You're going to feel better and this is going to be so much fun."

The drug takes effect almost immediately. Her eyes soften and a dazed look fills them. She remains conscious, just enough. I practiced the dosing on myself many times, getting it just right. I know she feels fluid and swirly, but still here.

I pick up the knife and go to her.

She tries to push my hands away, but the drug has taken her strength.


Shadows have crawled up the pale blue walls.

"I have to go out for a while, my love." Rachel struggles to focus her eyes. A strange noise comes from her lips as she tries to form words.

"Don't even think of screaming. No one will hear you."

She blinks several times in rapid succession, makes sounds that resemble words. She pushes awkwardly into the corner again.

"Fine, if you don't want to play nice."

I wrap duct tape around her wrists and across her mouth. She feebly tries to push me away. "You're so cute. Now stop that." I press her into the bed, cover her with the bedspread. "I'm going out to get you a friend. She is a gift to you, because you deserve it."

Her eyes plead with me, clear and focused now. The bedspread nearly covers her face, I slide it down a bit, make her more comfortable.

"Don't worry, she won't be staying long. She will be fun, though. Soon it will just be you and me forever." I place a tender kiss on her forehead. "I'm so glad you're here."

# Chapter 22

## GABBY

"Wow, you look great!" Preston says at the door.

I smile shyly, pleased at the compliment, glad I went to the effort. I grab my jean jacket off the peg inside the door, slide it on and take my thin black gloves out of the pockets.

I look at the gloves and then shove them back in my pockets. Tonight I want to feel things.

"Have you ever been to a corn maze before?" I ask on the drive out into the country.

"No. I've heard of them, but haven't gone. This one's supposed to be great, isn't it?"

"It's pretty famous. There's more than just the maze.

There's a smaller maze for the little ones, a straw bale pyramid to climb and games to play. There's even pumpkins and stuff for sale."

"I take it you've been more than once," Preston teases.

"My parents used to take Dustin and me when we were young.   I always got my face painted like a pony princess.   I loved it." I stare out the window and force away the memories of our family before my father was murdered.    That was another life, and I was another person then. "I hear it has grown a lot since then.   More like a festival now."   I force cheer into my voice. "But watch out, I might still get my face painted as a pony princess."

"And I might get mine painted too," Preston joins in. "I'm thinking a tiger, though."

I look at the man beside me, enjoying his quirky humor, thankful for the friend.

"How exactly do they make a maze in the corn? Do they mow it or something?" Preston asks.

"Not quite. Early in the summer, the owners plant the field and then remove the baby corn plants to make the maze pattern.   After the corn grows tall, a series of paths is left that can only be seen from the air.   Later in the fall, after the maze season, they harvest the corn as usual and the owners begin planning for next year's maze. Kind of ingenious, really.   Each year the pattern is different."

"Think we'll get lost?"

"That's part of the fun."

Judging by the number of cars in the parking area, this

year's maze must be a hit. We find an open space at the far corner of the dirt lot. Halfway across the lot, walking on uneven ground, I remember why I rarely wear my ankle boots. The low heels are not made for fields, but I have to admit they look good.

The crowd overwhelms me as we enter through the gates. The lights of the food vendors and booths are like islands in the dark of the fields surrounding us. I feel exposed without my gloves on, cross my arms over my chest. Every innocent glance at us increases my anxiety. "They're not talking about me, they're not judging me," I say in my head.

"Look, they have lemonade shake-ups," Preston says, oblivious to my inner thoughts. His obvious excitement calms my nerves. "Want one?"

I force my arms back to my sides, and let a smile cross my face. "Maybe later."

"Is that the maze?" Preston points to an opening in the field, with a large sign next to it with a map of this year's maze.

We study the outlines of animals connected with paths.

"This thing is huge, a lot bigger than I imagined," Preston says.

"Scared?" I tease. "They have a smaller maze over there for the kids."

"Nice try. Let's go."


It only takes a few moments for the bustling sounds of the main area to fade away. The dry corn stalks reach over our heads, blocking out the few stars above. A gentle breeze rustles through the corn, shaking the leaves in a timeless scratching song.  We turn down a path and are quickly alone in the corn.  We wander along in companionable silence, making turns at random.

"Any idea where we are?" I ask.

"I think we're lost already."

"That's part of the fun." I lean closer to him, catch a whiff of his cologne.  "That's why you brought me here, isn't it, to get me alone?" My daring attitude feels good.

"You saw right through me, didn't you?"

He slides his hand into my bare one.

The touch of skin on my usually gloved palm hits in a jolt. The intimacy of the simple act makes my breath catch.

His long, thin fingers squeeze gently.

I almost pull away.

I choose to squeeze back.

We continue walking, talking now and then. Any thought of solving the maze far from my mind, I focus only on the man next to me, the warmth of his hand in mine.

Too soon, the lights of the main area glow in the sky over the corn, and we near the exit.

"Looks like we almost made it out," he says.

"Guess we're just that good," I say lightly, my steps slowing to match his.

A group of people hurry past us towards the exit.

Preston suddenly pulls me into the corn, a few rows away from the path, a universe away from the world.

His body nearly touches mine as he stands facing me.

The leaves from the corn push against us on all sides. My right hand is still in his. He runs his other hand down my left arm. I tense slightly. He stops at my wrist and holds it gently.

"Now you really do have me alone," I say breathlessly.

The heat from his body fills the tiny space between us.

"Do you mind?" His breath brushes my cheek. I lean into him, close the space between us.

"Does it look like I mind?"

Releasing my hand and wrist, he slides his arms around my back, catches my hair gently. My own arms pull him closer still.

Hidden by the shadows, his lips hesitate just beyond mine, testing, waiting.

The moment stretches, unbearable in its sweetness. His lips finally meet mine, a gentle brushing, followed by a firmer insistence.

I melt into the pleasure of the kiss, give into the glory of his touch.

An electric stab of pain courses through my left forearm.

# Chapter 23

## GABBY

Preston pulls away, startled by my cry of pain.

I let go and hold my arm against me. The initial shock that coursed through my cross tattoo has faded, but an insistent buzzing burns below my skin.

"Gabby?" he asks, confused.

"I'm sorry, my arm is-." I don't know how to finish the thought. No one knows about God talking to me through my tattoo. Preston has been so sweet and understanding, I don't want to ruin things with him.

He tries to take my arm, look it over for an injury, concerned.

I snap my arm away.

The buzzing continues, a matching buzz fills my mind. I look over my shoulder, desperate to follow the call.

"I have to go." I stumble through the corn rows, back to the main path.

Preston follows me into the relative light of the path. "What's going on?"

"Please, just trust me. I have to go do something." I look down the path, back into the maze. The urge to go overpowering. I take a few steps back into the maze.

Preston tries to follow me.

"You can't come with me." Desperation fills my words. "Go get us a lemonade shake-up." I walk backwards, desperate to get away. I rub my arm, try to stop the burning buzz. "Wait for me. I'll be right back."

I turn and hurry down the path, into the maze. Preston calls after me, but thankfully doesn't follow.

A turn in the maze and I'm finally alone. I focus on the call, closing my eyes and tipping my head to get a read on where I'm needed.

I don't stop to think of the absurdity of the situation. I only obey.

Heading down the path as quickly as possible in my ankle boots, I make turns while listening to the call. The lights of the main area fade far behind me as I move deeper into the far corner of the maze. The path eventually turns into a dead end. My only choice is to turn around, and try another path, but it doesn't feel right. I stand and listen, open my mind to God, even raise my hands, palm up, listening beyond the scratching of the corn leaves.

Nothing.

Pulled by an invisible force, I step off the path, into the corn. I push against the leaves, slide between the stalks, searching.

In the darkness, I trip over her.

Stalks break off as I cling to them for balance. I fall hard on the ground, corn tumbling down around me. The broken stalks allow pale moonlight to filter in,

193

illuminating the young woman laying face down between the rows.

I scramble to the body, praying for her to be okay.

Her skin is warm.

As gently as possible, I turn her over. She moans and tries to swipe me away.

Tears of relief slide down my cheeks.

"You're okay. You're okay." I try to soothe as she wakes up. Hearing my voice, she stops trying to fight me off. I hold her head on my lap, and keep talking to her.

Her eyes flutter open.

"Where am I?" she creaks out.

"At the corn maze. You were unconscious. Don't try to move. Just rest a minute."

She takes a few moments to compose herself. She looks young, maybe eighteen. Fully conscious, she sits up. "What happened? Ouch, my head hurts." She rubs her throat.

"I don't know. I just found you laying here. What do you remember?"

"I was with my friends. I ran ahead and was going to scare them." She looks around suddenly. "Where are they?"

The young woman cocks her head. "I hear them."

In the distance, voices call out, "Melanie! This isn't funny. Melanie!"

"Over here!" I call out for her. "Melanie's over here."

Melanie stands up, a little disoriented.

"Let's get you back to the path." I carefully lead her then yell for her friends again.

"What happened after you ran ahead?"

"I don't know. Maybe I passed out or something. We have been drinking." She looks sharply at me. "You won't tell anyone will you? My parents will kill me."

I ignore her irrelevant fear. "Did you see anyone? Did someone do something to you?"

Melanie looks at me surprised. "Do you think someone did something to me?"

"It just seems odd you would suddenly pass out. We should call the police. " I don't want to scare her, but the whole thing feels off.

"No police! I just passed out. It's the only thing that makes sense." Melanie looks me in the eye, desperate to believe the story she's telling herself.

"Melanie, listen-." Just then three teenage girls descend upon us.

"There you are!"

"That wasn't funny."

"We've been wasting all this time looking for you."

The girls talk over each other.

"We're supposed to be going to Josh's party, remember?" the girl with the darkest hair adds, obviously annoyed.

"Sorry, I, uh," Melanie looks at me, pleading with her eyes.

She suddenly looks so young. I remember what it was like, wanting so badly to fit in.

"Melanie was helping me out," I say. "Sorry I kept her so long."

The dark haired girl looks me up and down, a hard set

to her shoulders. "And who are you?" she snarks.

"I'm Gabby McAllister." I reach out my hand as if to shake hers, playing along. The girl ignores my hand and I drop it back to my side.

"You're that crazy psychic lady everyone's been talking about."

"Guilty as charged," I say with a smile.

The dark haired girl loses interest in me and turns to her friends. "Come on, if we hurry Josh might still let us into the party." She turns on her heel and stalks off. The other two friends dutifully follow with Melanie close behind.

I put a hand on her arm to stop her, but she pulls away. "I really think you should call the police and file a report. You might have been attacked."

"No way. Look, thanks for your help, but nothing happened." She rubs her head again. "Except I think I lost my necklace." She feels around herself, more concerned about the missing necklace than what happened to her. "I know I had it on earlier."

"Melanie, come on or we're going without you!" Dark-haired girl barks.

Melanie shoots me a quick look, then hurries off with her friends into the maze.

I can't brush off the situation as easily as she can. Melanie was in danger, I'm certain of it. God called me to her for a reason, a very insistent call. Someone attacked her and knocked her unconscious.

Taking out my cell phone and turning on the flash light function, I go back to where I found her. Even with my light, I can't find anything suspicious. The stalks I broke when I fell litter the ground, but there isn't a sign of a struggle. If Melanie doesn't remember anything, maybe she never had a chance to struggle.

I scan the ground for her missing necklace, knowing it's a long shot. I don't find it.

Not knowing what else to do, I kneel next to where I found her. I say my usual prayer, "Lord, let me see what I need to see." I stretch out my bare hand and place it on the ground where I found her.

Prepared for something to come, I'm surprised when I feel nothing. I force my mind to open, to see, but still nothing comes.

Discouraged, I sit and listen to the rattle of the corn. The corn keeps its secrets.

With Melanie long gone, and my powers oddly silent, I give up and trudge back along the path alone. I wander in the general direction of the entrance, not sure exactly which way to go. In my blind hurry to find Melanie, I didn't pay attention to the maze. When I came through with Preston, we saw several people. It's much later now, and I see no one.

A tingle of fear slides up my back as the wind picks up. I wrap my jean jacket closer to fight off the chill and the fear. "Don't let your imagination run wild," I tell myself outloud.

A few more random turns and I stop, confused. I scan the sky for the lights from the main area. A faint glow shows far to my right, the opposite direction I have been walking in. I face the lights and hope for the best.

Footsteps crunch behind me.

I turn, expecting to see another group of people still out.

The path is empty and the footsteps have stopped.

"Just your imagination," I mutter again and keep walking.

The footsteps crunch again. I don't stop, but listen intently. Someone is definitely close by.

I spin around suddenly, hoping to catch them.

A shadowy figure jumps off the path into the corn.

"Who's there?!" I shout with more courage than I feel.

The figure doesn't answer.

"I saw you. I know you're there. Why are you following me?"

The corn parts, and a figure steps onto the path. In the pale moonlight, I can't make out details, but I recognize the hooded jacket and hideous clown mask.

My body shakes, but I force my voice to be steady. "What do you want? Leave me alone."

"Did you find my gift?" his voice unnaturally low and menacing. It's obvious he's disguising it.

"Your gift?"

"I wanted you to find her dead, but you interrupted me."

I take slow steps away from the man. "That's not a nice gift. I prefer flowers."

My glib response seems to catch him off guard. I take advantage of his confusion, and run.

I plunge down the path, heading in the direction I thought I saw the lights of the main area. His footsteps pound behind me, steady.

He laughs as we run. A sick guttural sound, muffled by his hideous clown mask.

Adrenaline pumps through me, making me lightheaded with the rush. My legs burn, but I push on, thankful for the hours of running I do at the park. But the park path is flat, and I wear running shoes. My ankle boots and the uneven ground eventually do me in.

A large clod of dirt catches my boot heel. I slam face first into the ground, knocking the air from my already burning lungs. I gasp, trying to pull in oxygen.

The man leaps on my back, his knee pushing into my rib cage, making it even harder to breathe.

He grabs my hair and slams my face into the dirt.

Pain explodes between my eyes. He lifts my head by the hair, holds me there.

"You think you can run away from me? Nice try," he hisses in my ear. His voice is still forced low and gravelly, unnatural.

Hot blood runs from my nose, across my upper lip and drips on the dirt below me. The dark spots glisten in the moonlight.

The sight of my own blood, drawn by this mad man, ignites a fury.

I slam my head back fast, crashing into his face so near my ear. He lets out a howl of fury, and releases my hair.

"You witch!"

I roll sideways and he slides off my back.

I scramble away, dragging backwards, pulling myself in a half crab-walk.

He reaches for my feet and I kick him away. He reaches again, grabs my ankle. I kick against his chest with my other heel. My boot slides off in his hand and I'm free.

In a flash, I'm on my feet and sprinting as fast as I can with one foot in a sock the other in a heeled boot.

I ignore the paths this time, crash straight through the corn towards the light growing brighter on the edge of the field.

The dry leaves and ears of corn reach out like menacing hands, scratching my face, pulling at my clothes. Random stones stab my shoeless foot. I ignore the pain and run on.

The man chases close behind, panting and angry.

The lights grow closer, and I can hear voices and sounds of fun ahead.

My lungs burn, my nose aches and my feet are sore, but I push on.

Through the gaps in the corn, I see the lights. The edge of the field grows closer.

A few more steps and I will be free.

His hand makes a desperate grab and catches my jean jacket.

I scream and scream, hoping someone will hear over the sound of the crowd.

"Got ya!" he growls.

A quick twisting move, and my jacket slides off in his hand.

"Help me!" I scream and break out of the corn on the edge of the lights from the main area. I stumble in my one boot, and hit the grass hard, knocking the wind out of me in a tight clutch on my chest.

A few people mill around the main area, seeming far away. No one sees me, no one has looked in my direction.

"Get him! He's right behind me!" I croak out from my place on the ground, trying to make words and catch my breath at the same time.

No one turns.

The corn crashes behind me.

I scramble across the grass on my hands and knees, desperate to escape.

The crashing fades away, taking the clown-faced man with it.

I sink to the ground. Grass blades poke against my face, the smell of earth and my own blood fills my painful nose.

A man I recognize finally steps from the crowd towards me. I'm so relieved to see him, I don't wonder at his appearance or remember I'm mad at him.

# Chapter 24

## DUSTIN

"I still don't understand why you want to go to the corn maze," Alexis says for the third time tonight. "Walker's too young to do any of the activities."

"I want to do something as a family tonight," I answer again.

Alexis pauses in getting Walker into his car seat and eyes me skeptically, not buying it. "Why are we going so late? It's already Walker's bedtime."

"Are you sure you're not the detective in the family?" I slide closer to her, as she tucks a blanket over Walker in his seat. I put my hands on her hips, pull her close.

"Don't try to distract me. I know you're up to something." She leans into my touch to let me know she

203

isn't actually mad.

"We need to go. Lucas is meeting us there in half an hour."

"Lucas is meeting us? Now I know you're up to something." She kisses me on the cheek. "Okay, I'll play along. But you're buying me an elephant ear."

Walker is sound asleep in his seat when we arrive. He really is too young to enjoy most of the activities, but I feel cheated out of quality time with my son just the same. We snap his seat into the stroller and push him along with us.

Lucas is already there, walking around scanning the crowd.

"Have you seen her?" I ask as he approaches.

"No. Haven't seen the neighbor guy either. She might still be in the maze, although most everyone has come out by now."

"Seen who?" Alexis asks.

"Gabby," Lucas says.

Alexis stiffens. "So, when you said family time, you meant with her?"

"Not exactly. We just need to keep an eye on her and she's supposed to be here on a date," I try to explain.

"Gabby's a grown woman, Dustin. She doesn't need you and Lucas following her around." The anger in her voice surprises me.

"Someone tried to break into her house last night. We just want to make sure she's safe," Lucas answers for me, his tone stiff and controlled.

"By stalking her?"

"We aren't stalking her, just looking out for her," I try to placate my wife. "Look, we're here, together, let's just enjoy ourselves, okay."

Alexis purses her lips. "You should have told me what we were doing." She breaks into a smile. "I'll forgive you if we get elephant ears."

"You and your elephant ears." I take her hand. "We will keep an eye out over by the food, you keep watching the exit," I say to Lucas.

"You aren't really mad, are you?" I ask Alexis as we stroll along with sleeping Walker.

"No. I just don't understand why you had to bring Walker and me too if you are 'working'."

"I wanted to spend time with you. I've been so busy with this case, I've barely seen you guys. Is that so bad?"

"Not when you put it that way." She leans against me playfully.

We sit at a picnic table eating elephant ears, the sugary dough a rare treat on the diet Alexis has me on. The crowd has thinned to scattered groups of young people and couples sitting together. I nod at a few people I recognize. I don't see Gabby.

A man sits alone at a table, watching the exit nervously. He fiddles with a lemonade shake-up cup. He's turned away and I can't see his face. Something about his demeanor catches my attention.

"She probably isn't even here," Alexis speaks up suddenly, licking sugar from her fingertips. "Who goes to the maze on a date?"

"*This* is a date, remember?" I turn to her and give her a wink.

"You know what I mean." She tosses the empty plate in the trash.

"This is where she said she was going." I shrug, handing her a napkin.

"They probably changed their minds and went somewhere else."

"Yeah, maybe. Or they left already." I look back to the nervous man. His empty cup sits on the table, but he is gone.

"We could buy the pumpkins while we're here," Alexis suggests, motioning to the booths of fall decorations.

I scan the area again, pushing the stroller towards the booths.

Alexis takes her time looking over each item, asking for my opinion. I answer absently, feeling impatient. Gabby's not here. Walker isn't even awake to enjoy anything. Now I'm stuck shopping. Damn Lucas and this idea.

Walker lets out a squall, startling me.

"I'll get him," I say to Alexis, her hands full of pumpkins and dried corn.

Walker squalls again as I lift him from the stroller. He buries his tiny head into my neck, and screams into my ear. The scent of his hair fills my nose, along with the unmistakable smell of a dirty diaper. His warm body wiggles against my shoulder.

"Here," Alexis reaches for him, her purchases stowed

in the stroller. I turn him over to her reluctantly. Walker cries out again, then settles down once in his mother's arms. A twinge of jealousy spikes, but I tamp it down.

Now that Walker is quiet, I can hear the commotion.

"McAllister!" Lucas yells over the crowd insistently.

Alexis and I lock eyes.

"Go," she says simply, just the barest hint of annoyance in her voice.

I push through a crowd of people gathered at the far edge of the main area.

Blood and dirt cover my sister's face. Lucas helps her hobble to a nearby table.

"What happened to you?" I rush to her side.

She settles heavy onto the bench of the nearest picnic table. Her eyes search my face. Gabby's usual guarded expression is replaced with terror.

"He's out there still. In the corn. Go get him!"

"Who's out there? Who did this?" I ask.

"Where's your date?" Lucas asks at the same time.

"The clown mask man. The same one from last night. Please, Dustin, he's so close. He attacked a girl and then he attacked me. Go get him."

Her words make no sense, but her fear is tangible. I look at Lucas, reluctant to leave Gabby, but needing to find the attacker.

Alexis appears. "I'll look after her." Baby wipes in hand, she crouches by Gabby.

Without a word, Hartley and I head into the cornfield. I reach for my pistol, then realize I don't have it. This was supposed to be a nice family outing, not a man hunt.

Lucas has his in hand.

We split up to cover more ground. A few minutes in the dark corn and the futility of our search crashes over me. There's no way to find one man in these acres of corn in the dark. There's a thousand places he could be and I can only see a few feet in front of me.

I stand and listen, hoping to hear him crashing around, hoping to hear anything.

"Gabby?" a man's voice calls in the distance. I give up hunting for the clown man, hoping Lucas has better luck, and head towards the voice calling for my sister.

I find him on a path near the center of the maze.

"Hey," I shout at him. "Police, don't move."

The man freezes, puts up his hands even though I didn't ask him to.

I recognize him as the nervous man from earlier.

"What are you doing out here?" I ask, more harsh than I really need to be.

"I'm looking for my date. She told me to wait for her, but she's been gone for a long time."

The man still has his hands up. I let him stand there like that.

"Are you Preston?" He nods, confused. "Why did you let her go alone?"

"She told me she had something to do and to wait for her. She didn't give me a choice." An edge of defensiveness in his voice.

I sigh, sounds like typical Gabby behavior. "You have no idea what she was doing or where she went?"

"No, I didn't. Look, what's going on? Are you really

208

the police?"

"I'm Detective Dustin McAllister." I wait, wondering if he will recognize my name.

"Gabby's brother." Preston lowers his hands. "Is Gabby alright? I can't find her."

"She's at the front. She was attacked by someone."

Preston scans the sky, finds the lights of the main area and takes off through the corn.

# Chapter 25

## GABBY

Dustin and Lucas run into the field, leaving me alone with Alexis. My bare hands shake and my blood pulses painfully in my ears. Alexis wipes gently at my face with baby wipes after she calls in to the police station. Her voice is calm and steady, the voice of a police wife.

My voice stutters. "He attacked a girl," I stammer. "I found her unconscious. He said he wanted me to find her dead, but I interrupted him."

"Shhh, don't talk now," she says in a voice I assume she uses with Walker. My nephew sits in his stroller, playing with a toy, oblivious to the drama going on around him. His innocence a stark contrast to the evil I just escaped from.

I touch my nose and wince. It hurts, but I don't think it's broken. Alexis being so close to me sets my already rattled nerves on edge. I don't remember even being alone with my brother's wife before. The warmth of her hands on my cheeks and her tender administrations feel alien and uncomfortable.

I reach to pull her hand away from my face, touching her wrist with my bare hand.

She pulls away as if I shocked her.

This reaction feels more familiar, almost comforting in a strange way.

She has the good grace to look ashamed of her action. I choose to ignore it and take the wipe from her hand and finish wiping blood from my own face.

Alexis stands and takes a barely perceptible step away from me.

A small crowd has gathered around us, curious stares, but no offers to help.

I concentrate on my breathing and watch Walker's cute antics. I block out everything else.

Several long minutes later, someone crashes out of the corn. I jump involuntarily, ready to run.

It's Preston, his face stricken.

"What happened? Are you okay?" His questions fire out faster than I can answer them. He has no qualms about touching me and pulls me into an embrace as soon as he reaches my side on the bench. I allow myself to melt into his arms, the small tether of my control slipping.

Preston pulls me so close he accidentally bumps my sore nose and I make a small sound of pain.

He pulls away, "I'm sorry. Did I hurt you?"

"My nose."

He touches my cheek gently, wiping at a spot of blood I missed. "You're a mess," he says.

Dustin stalks out of the corn. Even in plain clothes, the set of his shoulders and the way he walks screams cop. Fury in his eyes, he turns on Preston.

"You want to tell me where you were when Gabby was attacked?" Dustin growls.

Preston stands quietly. "I was waiting up here for her. I already told you that."

"Convenient story."

"True story," Preston counters.

Lucas approaches the verbal standoff, something in his hand.

I nearly scream when I see the clown mask he carries.

"I found this at the edge of the field. The guy's gone, though." Taking note of my reaction, he hides the mask out of my line of sight. "I see we found the missing date." His tone leaves no doubt he has the same opinion as Dustin.

"This is ridiculous, Preston didn't attack me," my stammer gone.

"Just a coincidence he was there both times you see this clown guy?" Lucas asks, stepping next to Dustin.

"I would never hurt Gabby." Preston states simply. The other two men are taller and broader than he is, but Preston stands his ground admirably against them. I

213

struggle to my feet to stand next to him.

"I was with Preston when the girl got attacked." I state. "He didn't do it."

"Tell us about this girl. Where is she now?" Dustin asks.

I tell them about finding Melanie unconscious and how she didn't believe anything happened to her. "She left with her friends. She didn't want me to tell anyone."

"And how exactly did you find this 'girl' in all this corn?" I don't like Dustin's tone. I've heard it many times over the years.

The crowd of people seem to lean closer, listening to my story. Preston looks at me intently, curious as well. I can't find the words, can't explain.

"I-." My stammer returns. Nervously, I rub my tattoo under my sweater, even though it isn't tingling.

Dustin sees the small movement and makes a disgusted noise.

"Let me guess, you sensed it?" His words drip with sarcasm.

I lock eyes with my brother, oblivious of the people around us. "Yes, I did. I sensed it and I went to her. Good thing I did, too, or else she would be dead." No trace of stammer, each word clipped and clear. I glare at Dustin, daring him to contradict me. He holds my eyes as the moment stretches, then looks away. Victory to me.

I look around the group, all eyes staring at me in open curiosity.

Suddenly, exhaustion climbs over me. My nose hurts, my bones hurt, my heart hurts. I need to get away.

"Preston, please take me home." I force as much strength into my voice as I can.

Preston stares at me, hesitates. Just a tiny hesitation, but enough to cut me. I turn and walk away and he follows a few steps behind.

"We aren't done questioning him," Dustin calls after me.

I spin around. "Yes you are. You go do whatever police work you need to find this guy who attacked me and Melanie. Preston and I are leaving."

I'm sure Dustin has more to say, but I'm not listening.

I struggle along with my one boot. Frustrated, I pull the boot off and throw it across the parking area. Stones poke my bare feet, but I don't care. I pull the door handle of Preston's car. It's locked. Preston presses the button on his key fob and the lock pops up.

I climb in the car and slam the door.

He slides into the driver's seat next to me. Silently starts the engine and pulls out of the parking area towards home.

"Do you want to go to the ER and get your nose checked out?" Preston asks cautiously.

"I just want to go home and be alone," I sulk.

I can feel Preston thinking, deciding. "Do you want to talk about how you found the girl? What did he mean by 'you sensed it'?"

I sigh heavily, the bone tired feeling pulling me down. "I don't want to talk about it."

Preston visibly tenses next to me. "Right. Why would

you want to tell me about it? You only almost got killed because you didn't tell me before." I'm not sure how I expected him to react, but his anger catches me off guard.

We ride in silence and I stare out the side window, getting as far away from him as possible. What does he want from me? It's bad enough he knows about me seeing things with my touch. If I tell him God talks to me through my tattoo, he will never want to see me again. My own brother can't handle it.

The tension in the car grows as I don't respond. I swim in it, drowning in the misery of him so close, yet miles away. We turn down our street, our homes quickly approaching.

Time ticks by, marked by the mailboxes we pass. I sneak a glance at him. His jaw juts in hard anger, his lips clenched in an unfamiliar line.

The moment for honesty rushes to me, then passes. He pulls into his driveway next to mine and the moment slips away.

He climbs out of the car and slams the door behind him, leaving me alone in the empty space.

I get out, unsure what to do.

"Preston?" I offer quietly to his back as he walks to his front door.

He stops, but doesn't turn around.

"One of these days, you will need to learn to trust someone."

"But-."

"When you decide to trust me, you know where I live. Good night, Gabby."

Preston goes through his front door. It clicks shut with a small, sad sound. I stand barefoot and alone on his driveway, nothing but the dark to keep me company.

# Chapter 26

## GABBY

This evening started with so much promise and now it lays in shambles. Without my shoes and jacket, I shiver in the night air. I let myself into my house, check on Chester and roam from room to room, unsettled. I peel off my tight jeans and sweater and replace them with loose, comfortable clothes. The weary feeling still pulls me down, but I don't want to go to bed. I feel caged and vulnerable alone in my tiny house.

A few minutes later, I turn the key in the Charger and roar out of the driveway. I speed away from Preston, away from the fear of my own home.

I drive too fast down back roads, Twenty-one Pilots blasting so loudly my ears ring. No matter how fast I drive, the pain stays with me.

I want my mother, but that's not possible. She's locked

away for a crime she didn't commit. Locked away from her life and locked away from us.

Eventually, I pull into Grandma Dot's gravel driveway. The windows in the old farmhouse stand black and empty. Her old flatbed truck isn't in the driveway, and I remember it's her bowling night. I park anyway. This is the only home I have left that feels safe.

I let myself into the kitchen. Jet yaps from his kennel, at first in warning, then in excitement once he realizes it's me. At least the small dog wants to see me. I let him out of the kennel and he dances around my ankles in a black fuzzy blur.

"Hey, Jet. Glad to see you, too. Grandma still have a few beers hidden in the fridge?" I ask the tiny dog. "I could really use a drink tonight."

I find a stray can of beer in the bottom drawer and take Jet out on the wide covered back porch. He runs out into the yard to do his business and I snuggle into one of the oversized wooden rockers.

Enjoying the moonlight, I sit in the dark, taking heavy gulps of the bitter beer. I hide from the disappointment of Preston, hide from the disgust of Dustin and Alexis, hide from the inconvenience I am to Lucas.

Mostly, I hide from the fear of the man who wants to hurt me. Jet jumps up the steps, done with his activities in the yard.

"Come here, Jet." I coax him closer. He puts his front paws on my knees, something in his mouth. I take the bundle away from him, expecting one of his many toys.

A dead bird lays in my hand, its neck at an odd angle,

its feathers falling off into my lap.

Startled, I toss the dead thing away and hurriedly brush the feathers off of me.

The dead bird breaks me, and I sob. Heavy, choking sobs. Jet looks at me, a worried cock to his head. I gather the small dog to me, pull my knees up onto the chair and curl myself into a protective ball around him. I focus on his heartbeat against my palm, focus on the soft fur in my hands. I don't want to feel the pain, the loss, the loneliness. I don't want to feel at all.

Forcing the tears to stop, I chug the last of my beer. Welcome the slight swirl in my head from the unaccustomed alcohol.

I tuck my chin back into Jet and squeeze my eyes shut. A vision of a clown mask fills my mind.

I will my mind to emptiness.

The chair rocks slightly in the breeze, like the gentle hand of God. I take comfort knowing He is with me even if no one else is, and drift to sleep.

I wake to Jet struggling in my lap and the rumbling sound of an engine. Jet jumps from my lap and runs out to meet Grandma Dot's flatbed.

"Jet, what are you doing out here? Why is Gabriella's car here?" she asks the dog. I can hear the concern in her voice all the way from my seat on the porch.

"I'm here, Grandma." I call to her.

"What happened?" she asks, getting right to the point.

"Good to see you too," I try to sound funny, but miss the mark.

She walks up the few steps, pauses to look at me carefully. "You need tea," she states simply.

I follow her into the kitchen, not sure what to say.

"You're a mess. Go get cleaned up and we can talk."

In the hall bathroom, I look at myself in the mirror. Dirt smears my cheeks. The mascara I so carefully applied earlier has run in dark streaks from my tears. Remnants of blood show below my nose. No wonder Grandma looked so worried. A mess is an understatement.

I wash my face and try to tame my wild curls. After making myself as presentable as possible, I re-join her in the kitchen.

I clutch the hot tea, and avoid her eyes.

"Want to talk about it?" she asks gently.

I shake my head, but the words tumble out anyway. Grandma Dot listens in her quiet way, perfected from years of listening to clients pour out their deepest secrets.

"I didn't feel safe at home, so I came here." I finish.

She takes a sip of her tea, her hand shaking as she lifts it to her lips. "You saved a girl from being murdered, and she didn't believe she was in danger. Then you get attacked and nearly killed and Dustin gets mad about you 'sensing' the danger for the girl. Not mad *you* were hurt. Alexis pulls away from you instead of helping you. Then this Preston gets mad at you for not telling him all your secrets on a first date? Do I have the story about right?"

"A little skewed in my defense, but that's pretty much it." Her quick defense of me soothes me more than the hot tea.

"I'm going to have to talk to that boy and his wife."

"No, please don't. I'm used to them. If you say something, it will only start more trouble."

"Fine, but one of these days I'm going to spank him. I don't care if he's a grown up cop or not." Grandma Dot winks at me. The image of her turning Dustin who's twice her size over her knee makes me smile.

"I'd love to see that." I giggle, glad for the tension relief.

"Now, forget about those jerks. The most important thing is your safety. Any idea who's after you?"

"None. It has to be whoever killed Karen and Steven. No one else would be after me so violently."

Grandma considers this for a moment, nodding absently. "So we have to figure out who killed them and get him locked up before he can get to you. Does Dustin have any leads?"

"They still think Patrick did it, although they haven't brought charges against him. I guarantee Patrick Jennings wasn't chasing me through the corn maze tonight."

"You said before it was someone they both knew and trusted. That limits the list."

"But I don't know anyone they both knew. I was just a little girl then. Do you have any thoughts?"

"Just that your mom ran in their crowd back then. Are you still going to see her tomorrow like usual?"

"Yes. Honestly, I'm looking forward to getting out of River Bend, even if it's just for a few hours. Whoever this guy is, he can't get to me in the prison. That sentence sounds absurd as I say it. What happened to my life? It used to be so boring and predictable."

"Gabriella, you've never been boring a day in your life."

"After this week, I'd welcome a little boring. At least for a day or two." I swirl the last of my tea in the bottom of the cup, then drink it down.

"Do you mind if I sleep here tonight?"

"I expected you would. You're always welcome here. This is your home."

Later, curled under the yellow bedspread in my old room, I think about Grandma Dot's words. Home. I haven't felt at home since before my father was murdered and my mother was taken away. Grandma Dot loves me and kept me safe here, the closest thing to home I will ever be able to have. The empty part inside me follows wherever I go. Even in my own house, it haunts me.

I drift asleep thinking of my mother, remembering her easy smile from the days before our life was torn apart. I can almost smell the coconut of her lotion, feel her hand touch my cheek. I can almost feel her tucking me in at night, whispering in my ear, "Good night, Gabby. I love you."

Almost feel her.

Almost.

# Chapter 27

## GABBY

I make the drive to the outskirts of Indianapolis every month to visit my mother in prison. Grandma Dot comes along with me when she can, but mostly I go alone. It hurts Grandma to see her only daughter in prison for something she didn't do. Her visits have gotten fewer and farther between as the years have passed. Dustin has never visited her. He has held fast in his belief she murdered our father, no matter what I tell him.

I'm nearly all my mother has now, and I take the responsibility seriously.

The heavy overcast sky that hangs over River Bend gives way to bluer skies as I drive south on I-69. The farther I get from home, the lighter my heart feels too.

The routine of my monthly visit grounds me.

I listen to my favorite podcast to keep me company. Crime Junkies fills my mind with stories of other murders. I listen closely, trying to find a clue or an idea to help me solve the mystery I'm stuck in. I don't find any.

I go through the security checks as smoothly as possible. I bring nothing with me, and wear only loose fitting, soft clothes. I know the drill. The fewer things they have to check, the easier it is.

The smell of disinfectant and stress-sweat surrounds me as I settle into the visiting booth. I sit on the plastic chair at the booth with a plastic window separating me from where my mother will soon sit. Handprints smear the Plexiglas, reminders of previous visitors desperate to touch. One leg of my chair is shorter than the other, and I fight the urge to rock it as I wait.

I don't have to wait long and my mother sits before me. A bright smile lights up her pale, thin face. Her eyes, the color of sky, an exact match to mine, look too big for her face. She tries to hide their haunted look with her smile. Her hair has grown since I last saw her, more gray at the roots than before. She looks old, nearly unrecognizable from the memories I fell asleep to last night. The realization frightens me.

The need to hold her and be held by her swamps me. The Plexiglas blocks any chance to touch, but I yearn for it anyway.

I remove the sticky phone from its cradle and hold it near my ear, but not touching it. I'm thankful for my gloves.

"Gabby," she breathes excitedly into the phone.

"Hi, Mom." I feel shy suddenly, not wanting her to see my need. "How are you?"

"Oh, you know the same as always," she says, a slight hint of sarcasm in her voice.

"Of course," I reply. I study her face, a little girl searching for comfort.

"Is everything okay, Gabby? You seem off. Is Dustin all right?" Her concern for the son she hasn't seen in twelve years makes me angry.

"Dustin is the same as always." I stuff down my resentment.

"And Grandma Dot?"

"Everyone is just the same, Mom." I run a finger along the counter, nervous. "Well, actually, I'm not the same."

"I can see that," she says gently. "What's going on?"

As clearly and concisely as possible, I tell her about the murders and my part in finding the killer. She hangs on my every word, no doubt the most exciting story she has heard in years. I gloss over the parts about the man after me, leaving out the terror I felt. I don't want her to worry. She's too far away and unable to do anything about it.

"You actually saw their deaths when you touched the bones?"

I nod.

"I knew you had the gift, as Grandma Dot calls it. I didn't know you could do that." I can't tell if her tone is disbelief or awe.

"I can do lots of things. I just don't talk about it." I dart

227

my eyes away, afraid of her reaction. We've never talked about the things I see. She knows the basics, but I don't tell her specifics. Of course Grandma told her some of it when I was younger.

"That's amazing!" Pride obvious in her voice. It rolls over me in a warm wave and the tension in my shoulders relaxes.

I shrug at the praise, but let her see in my face how much it means to me.

"Now I have a problem," I continue. "I vowed to prove Patrick Jennings' innocence, but I don't know how. Grandma said you ran in the same circles as both Karen and Steven back then. Maybe you could remember something. Someone they both knew and trusted."

"I wouldn't say we ran in the same circles exactly. Your father and I went to a few neighborhood parties and things, but mostly we kept to ourselves. It was a long time ago. Let me think."

Her eyes lose their focus as she thinks back to those years. "The only thing I really remember was Steven's daughter babysat for you and Dustin a few times."

"Rachel?"

"Yeah, sounds right." She sits lost in thought a few more moments. "Yeah, I remember now. We were looking for a new sitter, and Karen told us Rachel sat for her boys. Said she was great and really trusted her. So we hired Rachel to watch you kids a few times."

"That's it?" I had hoped for more than a babysitter recommendation as a connection.

"I'm sorry. It's the only connection I can think of."

228

"Rachel and her mom were out of town the night of the murders. I don't see how her babysitting for Karen's kids really helps us."

"I wish I could remember more. I'll keep thinking about it. I've got nothing else to do in here but think."

"I wish things were different, Mom," I say softly.

"Me, too. At least I get to see you every month." I catch the slight inflection on the word "you," and know she's thinking of Dustin. Rage at my brother fills me as it does every month. Mom doesn't belong in here, and the least he could do is visit.

"I'll always come, Mom. You can count on that."

"I can always count on you." Again the slight inflection, I'm sure she doesn't realize she's doing it.

"Is there anything you can tell me about that night? Any tiny detail you've remembered?" I hate the desperation in my voice.

"We've been over this a million times. I told everything to the detectives and to the defense attorney. It didn't help."

We sit thinking. Most of our visits end like this. Both of us wishing things could be different. Both of us powerless to change it.

"Put your hand on the glass. I want to try something." I slip off my glove and place my palm flat on the Plexiglas. She matches mine on the other side.

I close my eyes and concentrate.

*Fighting with Nathan, angry words that mean nothing. Driving, worrying. Empty country roads and loud music. Regret and return.*

*Kitchen covered in blood. Sliding through the slick. Gabby on the ground. DON'T BE DEAD! She's breathing, she's alive. Nathan where are you?*

Her fear for me slams raw and painful, and true. The shock of it makes me pull my hand away to break the connection.

"What did you see?" she asks in a scared voice, her hand still on the glass.

"What I've always known. You would never hurt dad or hurt me."

I slip my glove back on in disappointment. I'd hoped for some sign or clue or anything I can use to get her out of prison.

It's too late for her, but I can still clear Patrick Jennings. I can save Seth and Nicholas from sitting in a chair like this, unable to touch their parent. Save them from years of watching a loved one grow older and thinner, wasting away instead of flourishing.

Maybe saving Patrick will soothe my guilt from not saving my mother.

"Do you remember anything else at all about Karen and Steven? Or even Rachel or her mom?"

"I remember when they ran off together, of course. It was the gossip around town for weeks."

"That's what everyone has said." I scramble to think of another question, anything to help me figure out the case.

"I just remembered something, although it's tiny," Mom says.

My heart jumps, hopeful.

"One time while Rachel was babysitting, we came

home early. Her boyfriend was at our house."

"That's not much to go on."

She continues, "Tall skinny kid, with curly hair. I only remember because I didn't like the feeling I got from him. He was too eager to impress. Your dad and I called him Eddie Haskell, like from Leave it to Beaver."

The reference means nothing to me.

"Do you remember his actual name?"

"Uhmm, no." She searches her memory, trying to find the name. "Kind of dorky name, it fit him. I'm sorry, I don't remember. We never had her sit for us again."

"I can always ask Rachel. Of course her mom told me to stay away from her."

"Oh, and Patrick was a coach at the ballpark. Dustin had just started T-ball, and we used to see Patrick around with his boys. They were older and in a different league." She stops talking, thinking about the past. "That's right, that's where I met Karen. At the ballpark."

"Patrick was coaching the boys the night of the murders. It's his alibi."

"I guess that makes sense. Seems like we were at the ballpark a lot then. Dustin was so cute in his uniform. His hat was way too big on him and covered his ears. He hit the tee more than the ball, but he loved to run." The sad smile on her face nearly breaks my heart. My familiar anger at Dustin flares again.

The smile disappears suddenly and Mom looks over her shoulder, responds to the guard speaking to her.

"My time's up. Thank you for coming every month. I don't know what I'd do without your visits." Her words are rushed, trying to fit them in before she has to hang up. "Be careful, Gabby. I love you so much." She tosses in at the last moment before she hangs up and is led away.

"I love you, too, Mom," I say into my end of the receiver even though she has moved out of sight.

# Chapter 28

## GABBY

The drive home from the prison has the opposite effect as the drive down. The closer I get to River Bend, the stronger my dread grows. I yearn to turn around, just drive away. Maybe head south all the way to Florida and the beach.

I can't run away. I have work to do.

I contemplate calling Dustin and telling him off for hurting our mother. Maybe even confront him for the way he acted toward me and to Preston last night. I decide not to waste my breath. Dustin will always be what he has always been. A colossal pain in my butt.

The memory of Preston's kiss last night, pops into my head every few miles. So sweet and so tender. And so different from the way the night ended with me alone in the driveway.

Guilt and longing settle in. I owe him an explanation.

My call to him goes to voicemail immediately. I console myself that his phone is turned off, not that he declined my call. I don't leave a message, though.

My call to Seth gets picked up. I owe him an update on the case. It's only been two days since he hired me, but it feels like a lifetime.

"Hey, Seth, it's Gabby. Just wanted to check in with you," I say politely.

"Have you found out anything new?" The hope in his voice stabs me.

"Nothing concrete. I did talk to my mom today. She was friends with your mom and Steven's family. Unfortunately she didn't have anything useful to add."

"I know you're doing your best." Seth pauses. I can feel his indecision through the phone. "I heard a rumor you were attacked last night. Do you think it was him, the killer?"

"There's a small chance it's just some other nut job, but I feel certain it's the same man. None of the attacks started until I got involved in the case." I regret the words as soon as they leave my mouth.

"You got attacked because you're helping us?"

"That's not what I meant," I hurry to say. "Don't worry, I'll be fine. You just worry about your dad. I'll check back in with you tomorrow." I hang up before he can respond. I don't want to hear his concern or his guilt.

I make one more phone call on my drive home. This

one to Lucas, another friend I pushed away and made angry. I still don't understand what he and Dustin were doing at the corn maze last night. A bit too convenient to be a coincidence. A tiny piece of me hopes they were there to look out for me and keep me safe. Another piece of me rebels against the idea that I need protection. The largest piece of me says "get over yourself."

His phone rings a few times then goes to voicemail. This time I leave a message. "Lucas, it's Gabby. Talked to my mom today. She remembers Rachel Rawlings babysat for us as kids as well as for Karen's kids. I know it's not much of a lead, but I wanted to keep you in the loop. Oh and Rachel had a boyfriend at the time. Mom didn't know his name. Might want to look into that. Umm, thanks for your help last night." I stab the end call button on my phone, feeling like an idiot. Lucas probably already looked into it, he doesn't need me telling him what to do.

I sigh and turn on the Crime Junkies Podcast. I'd rather think about someone else's case for a while.


Preston's driveway is empty when I get home. I fight back the disappointment. I don't want to go into my empty house, but I have nowhere else to go and Chester needs some attention.

I lock and chain the door behind me and check all the windows to be sure they are locked as well. It's late afternoon, still several hours to fill before I can go to bed. I try to focus on a TV show, but my mind keeps wandering. I check next door a few times to see if Preston had come home yet, no car. I give in and call again, but still get voicemail. I chicken out and hang up.

What do I even want to say? Sorry I didn't tell you God talks to me through a tattoo on my arm? I'm sure that will go over well.

Finally I send a text. "Sorry about last night. I need to talk to you about it. I am going for a run now, but can we get together tonight?"

I hit send before I change my mind.

The caged feeling increases and I change into my running clothes and jacket.

Running tames my jumbled thoughts to a quiet swirl. I concentrate on my breathing, on my steps, on the pain in my legs. Frustration pushes my feet faster. My body finally gives in and I have to slow down. With a sharp stitch in my side, I walk through the parking area. The skewed angle of the Charger confuses me. On closer inspection, both my driver's side tires are slashed and sitting on their rims.

Fear shoots through me and my tattoo begins to tingle.

My eyes dart around the parking lot. A few other cars are parked nearby, but no suspicious man lurking in a clown mask.

I unplug the ear buds from my phone, ready to call for help. I don't know who to call.

Just then, a car pulls up behind me.

"Gabby, I thought that was you. You been running?" my boss, Herbert, asks through his rolled down window. Herbert may be annoying, but I welcome a friendly face.

"I was. But now my tires are flat."

Herbert cranes his head out the window to look at my tires. "They sure are. You need some help?"

"I only have one spare. I could call a tow truck or something."

"Or I could give you a ride somewhere. You can come back later to fix it."

I look from my slashed tires to his smile. "Sure, that would be great. Can you take me to my Grandma's? It's on the edge of town."

"No problem. Get in."

Alone with my boss in the small space of his car, I feel nervous and uncomfortable. We see each other every day at work, but we're not exactly friends. I search my mind for something to say. Herbert has plenty to say.

"How's the psychic thing going? Solve the case yet?"

I mentally roll my eyes. "Haven't solved it yet, but I'm working on it," I say casually. I'm planning what to do about my car. Do I buy new tires and take them to the car? Do I call a tow truck? How much is this going to cost?

I don't let myself think about who slashed them.

"You're so lucky to have that talent. It's very interesting." Herbert continues to gush, the way he did at work. The attention bothers me.

"Not sure I would describe it that way."

Herbert looks at me, studies me. "I would love to have that power." He watches me too long. Once he looks back at the road, he has to slam the brakes to make the red light.

A stuffed pig toy tumbles against my feet, sliding out from under my seat at the sudden stop. It looks familiar and I pick it up with my gloved hand.

"Oh, sorry about that. It's my nephew's. He loves pigs."

Suddenly, I remember where I saw the toy before. Regina's son has one.

"You're Regina's brother?"

"How'd you-? Oh, you're good." Herbert's smile is too wide.

My phone rings in my hand. I check the screen, hoping it's Preston. The screen says BLOCKED the way it does when my mom calls.

I drop the toy and accept the charges from the prison.

"Mom, everything okay?"

"Everything's fine. I just remembered the name of Rachel's boyfriend."

Herbert watches me intently, making me squirm. I rub my tattoo.

"Was it Herbert?" I ask, my eyes locked on my boss.

"How'd you know?"

The jolt from the stun gun stops me from answering. The electricity clamps painfully through my body. The pulse slams my head against the window.

My phone slips from my hand to the floor board. My mom's voice calling my name fades away.

"Didn't see that coming, did you?" Herbert's hiss chases me into the darkness.

# Chapter 29

## GABBY

"Wake up! You've kept Rachel waiting long enough." The words make no sense to me, but the slap across my face snaps me into consciousness just the same.

I raise my hand to touch the sting on my cheek, but my arm won't move. My wrists and ankles are duct taped to a chair. I jump and buck at the sight, trying to get away. The chair tips under me, teeters, then rights itself.

"There you are." Herbert leans close to my face, his hot breath blowing on my cheek. "About time you woke up. I promised Rachel a present, and you haven't been very cooperative."

Across the room, a blond woman huddles on a bed. Fresh duct tape covers her mouth. Outlines of sticky residue show where previous pieces of tape had been. A thin red line of a fresh cut mars her beautiful face. Dried blood streaks her cheek. Her wild eyes plead.

"Are you Rachel Rawlings?" I ask the woman.

She nods as tears roll down her cheeks causing the dried blood to smear.

Her tears spark primal anger in me. "How long have you kept her here?" I snap at Herbert.

"Don't blame me. You were supposed to be here last night, but you got away." Herbert looks longingly at Rachel. "No worries. We've kept each other company just fine."

Rachel shudders and cowers farther into the corner of the bed.

"What do you want?" My voice only quivers a little.

"You tell me, Gabby. You're the psychic." He waits expectantly, but I don't reply.

"Rachel and I are meant to be. I've known that since I first saw her in school." He turns his attention to the woman on the bed. "You were the most beautiful thing I'd ever seen. I couldn't believe you went out with me. Those months were the best time in my whole life. Well, up until the last two days with you."

Herbert sits on the edge of the bed. Rachel moves and a chain rattles under the blanket. The sound makes me sick.

"Then your dad tells you he's running away with Karen and you were so upset. He hurt you!" Rachel and I both jump at his sudden shout of anger. "I couldn't allow it. I took care of the problem for you, Rachel. I made them go away forever. You were supposed to lean on me, let me comfort you, realize I was all you had left." His voice trails off. He stands abruptly.

"Instead, you broke up with me."

Rachel makes some sounds, but can't speak.

He looks at her gently. "It's okay, now. We're together. The past is the past."

Herbert turns his full, sick attention on me.

"You think you're so special with your gifts. I bet you're a fake. Just a nosey woman who should stay out of things she doesn't understand. We're going to find out."

Herbert slides open a drawer, draws out a necklace. The chain glints in the light.

"Rachel deserves some entertainment, so we're going to play a game. Let's see if you're really what you pretend to be."

"What do you mean?" I stall.

"Touch this necklace and tell me what you see."

"That's sick."

"Said the fraud. What do you see?"

"I have to touch it. Undo my hand from the chair."

"Nice try."

I don't want to play, but will do anything to stall him until I can come up with a way to save us. "Then take off my left glove and put it in my hand."

Herbert slides my glove off with his fingertips, careful not to touch my skin. His fingers are long and unnaturally thin, a smear of red stains the base of his thumbnail.

He drops the necklace into my open palm.

I don't need to touch the necklace to know who it belongs to. Melanie said she lost hers last night. I close my eyes and focus anyway.

*Rattle of the corn, giggling quietly. Pain in the head. Too swift dive into darkness.*

I open my hand and toss the necklace as far as I can with my hand taped to the chair. It rattles to the floor. "That's from the girl you tried to kill last night."

Rachel makes a startled sound from the bed.

"Interesting," Herbert chuckles. "But that was an easy one. What do you think, Rachel? Have her do it again?"

Rachel closes her eyes and turns her head in answer.

He slides the drawer open again.

"Which one now?" he muses. "So many to choose from."

He takes a knit hat from the drawer.

"Try this one."

I refuse to open my hand again.

"Open your hand and play along, or I'm going to cut her. Again."

Rachel squeals. I open my hand and accept the hat.

I clench the fabric in my bare palm and say my prayer. "Lord let me see what I need to see."

The vision hits with a jolt.

*Audrey shivering with cold and need for a hit, warm car, clinging hands, revulsion, just get through it and get your money, slice to the skin, agonizing pain, another slice, and another.*

I force my hand open, dropping the hat and stopping the connection. I gasp for air, tears stinging my eyes. I scrunch them shut hard forcing the vision from my mind.

"So?" Herbert bounces with excitement, his evil eyes wide. "Did you see her?"

I swallow hard before I can make the words. "Her name was Audrey. You cut her." I keep my eyes shut tight to avoid looking at the monster before me.

"Well, done. Are you seeing this, Rachel? She's not a fake. Audrey never knew what was coming for her. Well, maybe towards the end she had an idea. Too late for her by then. She was a fun one."

The drawer scratches open a third time. He stirs among the items inside. He considers a moment, then makes his selection.

A bracelet this time.

He tries to hand me the jewelry. I shake my hand in refusal.

"Please, don't make me do it again," I plead.

He cocks his head and considers. "What do you think, Rachel? Should I make her do it again?"

Rachel shakes her head violently and tries to shout no from behind the tape. I lock eyes on the woman, feel her pain from across the room.

"Sadly, I only have a few more mementos. You can do it, Gabby. I believe in you now."

He forces the bracelet into my hand.

I drop it immediately.

"You're a spunky one." He retrieves the bracelet. "You were always so meek and quiet at work, never would have guessed you could be so entertaining. Do this last one, and then we can play another game."

The current game seems safer than what he has in mind for later.

He forces the bracelet into my hand.

"Now tell me what you see."

I struggle against the vision, not willing to see. I think of anything else, empty skies, endless waves on a beach. Against my will, the vision crinkles, then slides into focus.

*Janet on the side of the road, car trouble, thankful for help, driving into trees out of town, hard grip on her arm, running, panting, branches scratching and clinging at her, hitting the ground hard, weight on her back, blade at her throat, not happening, not happening, roll away, hand on the blade cutting to bone, push him away, cry of pain, slicing, stabbing, draining to dark.*

I drop the bracelet and kick it away with the toe of my shoe.

"You monster!" I scream. "You stabbed her and left her in the woods."

Herbert smiles proudly.

"Well done, Gabby. Holy crap this is cool! Janet was so much fun. She lasted a long time."

Vomit rushes up my throat and I turn to the side to puke. A vile splash on the wooden floor.

My mouth stings sour, my mind swims.

"Now you've made a mess," Herbert reprimands as if to a child.

I slump in my chair, exhausted and longing for emptiness. My head rolls to the side, my eyes closed. "God, please help us. Please." I beg silently.

"No-no. Come on and lift your head." He still talks like I'm a child. "Tell you what. One more and then you can take a break and rest up."

The sliding of the drawer again, my stomach roils.

"This is a good one."

I keep my eyes shut, go limp like I'm unconscious. My tattoo begins to tingle. I focus on the buzz, surprised. I open my tired mind, listen for the command as I've always done.

My tattoo burns, stings, insistent.

Herbert's trying to force something into my hand. "Come on now, this one's special. Take it."

I don't move.

"I said take it!" He slaps me across the face.

I spring awake, catching him off guard. Ignoring the lacey item he forces on me, I snap my hand around his wrist.

Our connection sizzles.

His face fills with fear, his mouth a dark "O" of surprise.

Rachel screams against her tape.

# Chapter 30

## LUCAS

The file on the murders spreads across my desk. I search each page again. I sigh heavily and lean back in my chair. I've been at it for hours, looking for something we missed. Gabby's attack last night and the intruder the night before have to be related to the case, which means whoever's after her must be in the file.

Dustin eyes me from his desk.

"Any luck?" He has duplicates of the file spread on his desk as well.

I shake my head. I'm still angry with him for the way he dismissed Gabby last night. If he wasn't my best friend and partner, I would have taken him aside and knocked him senseless.

I channeled my anger into something productive, finding the real killer and getting him away from Gabby.

At least I know she's safe right now. I talked to Grandma Dot this morning and she said Gabby went to see Emily in prison. Knowing she's not in town comforts me.

My desk phone rings, a welcome distraction from reading the same words over and over and getting nowhere.

"Hey, Hartley, a missing person's report just came in. The mother, Diane Rawlings, says she can't find her daughter Rachel. Hasn't been answering her phone since yesterday. Not at her house either, but her car's in the garage."

A sinking feeling pours over me. "The same Diane Rawlings and Rachel that are Steven Rawlings family?"

"Yep. Thought it might be connected which is why I'm giving it to you guys."

"I have her address right here on my desk. McAllister and I will head over to Diane's right now."

"What's up?" Dustin's already standing, ready to go.

"Rachel Skinner, daughter of Steven Rawlings is missing. Can't be a coincidence. Her mom called it in. Let's go talk to her."

We'd interviewed Diane Rawlings earlier in the week. An unpleasant experience. Her worry now hasn't improved her attitude any.

"We were supposed to meet for breakfast and then do some shopping today," Diane explains. "The kids are with her no-good ex. I already checked there. He said she dropped the kids off last night as normal."

"Did you try calling her?" Dustin asks the obvious question.

"Of course I did! I'm not stupid. She didn't answer."

"Just covering all our bases, ma'am," Dustin soothes.

"I went to her house to see if everything was okay. I have a key and let myself in. Everything seemed normal. Except she left an apple core and a soda can on the kitchen island. Rachel is normally very neat. Her car was in the garage, but she wasn't anywhere." Diane's voice cracks.

My phone buzzes in my pocket, but I ignore it and continue with my interview.

"What time were you at her house?"

"About an hour or so ago. After that I called her ex and then I called you. First Steven being found and now Rachel's missing." Diane breaks into tears.

We give her a few moments to compose herself. "Can you show us her house?" I ask.

"I already checked there, but if it will help find her, then sure."


Rachel's house looks undisturbed, just as Diane said it would be. The offending apple core and soda can are still on the counter.

"The core's dry and brown, looks like it's been here a while," I point out to Dustin.

"Probably not from this morning, then," he agrees.

"Here, I'll throw it away," Diane says.

"No, don't touch it."

Diane looks at me questioningly, then crumples. "This is a crime scene now, isn't it?"

"Until we find Rachel, it is," I answer.

"I'll call a team in to go over the house. Maybe they can find something we don't see," Dustin makes the call.

I take Diane back outside and tell her to go home and wait in case Rachel calls.

She reluctantly leaves, a last look over her shoulder as she drives away. Waiting is the worst part. I've been waiting for my sister to call for years.


In the last few hours, Dustin and I have supervised the techs at Rachel's house, who found nothing else interesting. We talked to the neighbors, all of which saw nothing.

Rachel simply vanished.

"Nothing more we can do here," Dustin finally says. "Let's grab a sandwich and head back to the station."

"Sounds good to me. You drive."

We place our orders at a drive through, neither of us saying much. As we wait for our food, I absently check my phone.

"I have a voicemail from Gabby," I tell him.

Dustin's shoulders tighten.

I listen to Gabby's message, a pit growing in my stomach. I put it on speaker and press repeat. "Listen to this."

"Lucas, it's Gabby. Talked to my mom today. She remembers Rachel Rawlings babysat for us as kids as well as for Karen's kids. I know it's not much of a lead, but I wanted to keep you in the loop. Oh and Rachel had a boyfriend at the time. Mom didn't know his name. Might want to look into that. Umm, thanks for your help last night."

"Can't be a coincidence she mentions Rachel and a boyfriend and now Rachel's missing."

Dustin pays for our food at the window and hands me the bags before replying.

"Nothing with Gabby is coincidence," he sighs. "When did her message come through?"

I check the timestamp. "A few hours ago."

Dustin pulls out of the drive-thru and into a parking spot. "Call Diane and ask her about this boyfriend."

Dustin opens his sandwich and wolfs it down in a few bites as I talk to Diane.

"Diane says Rachel dated a kid named Herbert Zinderman back in high school. Let's see if I can find an address." Using the computer in our car, I do an address search.

In a few moments, I have a current address and picture ID. "Dorky looking guy," I mention.

Dustin's own phone rings, cutting me off.

"It's Grandma Dot," he says as the phone continues to ring. We lock eyes then look away.

"This can't be good."

Dustin puts it on speaker then stabs the button to answer.

"Dustin? Something's wrong with Gabby!" Grandma Dot sounds hysterical, completely not her usual calm self.

"What's going on?"

"She went to visit your mother today and asked about some boyfriend or something."

"We know that part already."

"Well, Emily couldn't recall his name at the time, but she called Gabby a little bit ago to say she remembered. Gabby said she already knew his name. Then Emily said she heard Gabby make a strange noise and then nothing. The line wasn't dead, but Gabby didn't answer or say anything. Eventually the call hung up. Emily called to tell me, and now Gabby isn't answering me when I call. Something's wrong!"

"Was the boyfriend's name Herbert Zinderman?"

"Herbert something. That's all Emily could remember. Isn't Herbert Zinderman her boss?"

"Grandma, Lucas is with me. We'll find her. I promise."

Dustin hangs up, his face pale.

"Her house is on the way to Zinderman's. She might be just fine. Maybe she dropped her phone in the toilet or something." Dustin grasps, and I let him.

Her Charger's not in the driveway when we pull up and I feel sick.

"Let's ask her friend next door. Maybe he's seen her."

Dustin knocks hard on Preston's door, the insistent knock of the police.

Preston steps back quickly when he sees us on his step.

"What do you guys want? I told you, I didn't hurt Gabby last night. Even she told you that."

"This isn't about last night," I say.

"Have you seen her today? Talked to her?"

252

"No. I just got home from work. My phone was off all day. She did send me a text."

"Did she say where she was?"

"She said she was going for a run, but wanted to talk to me later. Why?"

I dial Gabby's number, hoping by some miracle she'll answer.

She doesn't.

"He must have her," Dustin says to me and we hurry back towards the car.

"Who has her?" Preston runs after us, catches me by the sleeve. "If Gabby's in danger, I want to know." Preston pleads with me.

"We think someone has her."

"The clown mask guy. You know who he is?"

I nod. "Let go of my arm so we can find her."

"I'm coming with you."

"No, you're not. This is police business."

"Gabby *is* my business. If you don't take me with you, I'll just follow you." I have to admire his dedication.

"Get in."

"We can't allow that," Dustin says.

"He's not giving us a choice."


Full dark envelops the run-down house at Herbert's address. No lights shine from the windows. The roof sags in the moonlight. Overgrown bushes swallow the porch. The front door hangs open at an odd angle.

"It looks abandoned," Dustin points out.

"This is the address he has on file," I reply. "He has to

253

be here with them." My blood sings with fear and disappointment. Gabby has to be here.

"Let's check it out." Dustin draws his gun and climbs out.

"Stay in the car," I tell Preston.

"Not a chance," he snaps. I admire his tenacity.

I hand him my club for a weapon. "Stay behind us."

We creep up to the house, listening for sounds, scanning for any sign of activity.

Quiet surrounds us. In the far distance, coyotes howl. Their song haunting in the dark.

A branch hangs over the steps to the porch. We push it aside and move on. We step carefully across the splintered porch, the wood creaking under our feet. A board gives way under my foot and I struggle to regain my balance.

Preston grabs the back of my jacket, steadying me. "Watch your step," I warn him.

The wooden door hangs open. One of the three panes of glass at the top is broken and shards litter the entry.

Dustin steps over the glass and pushes the door. It swings inward with a squeak of the hinges. The interior of the house yawns dark.

I motion for Preston to wait for us on the porch. He nods, his eyes so wide, I can see the whites in the moonlight.

Dustin goes in first, gun drawn and ready. Following close behind, we enter the house.

The smell of decay and animal waste assaults us. Small scurrying sounds come from the far corner of the room.

I switch on my flashlight and the scurrying increases. Mice dart away from the beam.

Leaves and trash litter the floor. Cobwebs hang in heavy dust-covered curtains.

"It's abandoned. They're not here." Dustin is crushed, desperate.

"Let's check it out anyway. Maybe we can find something to tell us where he lives now."

We clear each room and find nothing but more trash and mice.

Discouraged, we join Preston out front.

"There's no one here," I tell him quietly.

"Then what do we do now? We have to find them," Preston replies.

"He has to have them somewhere," Dustin says impatiently. "Let's check out the rest of the property." He strides around the side of the house into the back yard. Preston and I follow.

The tall grass tangles our feet and overgrown bushes dot the yard.

A gravel drive cuts along the side of the yard, barely visible in the weeds.

"There's a lane here," I shout to Dustin.

We follow the lane through a break in the surrounding trees and bushes.

"There's lights back there," Preston points to a trailer on the other side of the trees.

Hope jolts through us and we run silently towards the light.

A car sits next to the trailer.

"That matches the car he has registered in his name," Dustin whispers. "He's here. He must have Gabby and Rachel here too." Dustin's excitement matches my own.

We creep to the single lighted window.

A voice filters through the glass.

"Tell you what. One more and then you can take a break and rest up," a man's voice says.

I inch my head above the window sill and peek in.

Gabby slumps in a chair, her back to me. Her dark curls hang still. My whole body clamps at the sight of her motionless form. Blind rage dims my vision.

Her shoulders move with her breath and relief floods.

"She's here," I whisper to the others. "I don't see Rachel, just Gabby and Herbert."

Preston lets out a breath of relief.

Dustin sucks in a breath in preparation.

"Do you have a shot on him?"

"No. Gabby's in the way. I don't have a clear shot. Looks like she's tied to a chair."

"I'll go around to the front door. Preston, you stay here and do not move."

Dustin creeps away and I peek back in the window, hoping to get a clear shot at the monster.

The man slaps her across the face and I surge with anger again.

"I said take it!" he yells at her.

# Chapter 31

## GABBY

I clutch Herbert's wrist and a wave of anger and hatred and sickness pours into me like electricity.

Herbert can feel it too, and tries to pull away in shock.

I don't let go.

*Irrational hunger for blood, joy at death, longing for Rachel, desperation at his boring life, the love of the hunt...*

Herbert's inner thoughts pour through me, sicken me, drown me in darkness.

"Stop it!" he screams. "Let me go."

I open my eyes and look him straight in the face. The face I've seen for years at work. The man I ignored. The man overly eager for attention. But the man I knew was a mask, as much as the clown mask he wore to torment me.

I see the true man before me clearly in my vision. A broken, lonely shell of a human.

"I said let go, you freak."

He struggles against my grip.

My tattoo stabs, insistent.

Herbert wrenches his arm from my grasp.

The command in my mind screams *lunge forward.*

I obey.

The momentum of his pull and my lunge tumble me to the floor. My hands and legs taped to the chair, I can't brace my fall. I hit the wood floor with a heavy thud.

Herbert grabs his knife.

"You shouldn't have done that. Can't wait to see your blood."

He lunges at me, intent on cutting.

Taped to the chair, I can't move to save myself.

A gunshot pierces the room.

Glass shatters and rains across the floor. The smell of gunpowder fills the room, burns my eyes. My ears ring.

Herbert stumbles backwards, crumbles against the wall.

Rachel screams and doesn't stop screaming.

Blood splashes across his chest. He presses his hands to the wound, surprise twisting his face. He looks at the blood dripping from his hand. A sick expression of delight crosses his face.

He lays too close to me, but I can't move away.

"It's so beautiful," he murmurs.

He touches his chest again, smearing more blood on

his hand.

He holds it above him, delights in the drips as they splatter on his chest in tiny explosions of color.

"So wonderful, see?" He reaches towards me, wanting to share his wonder. He wipes the blood on my face, the sticky warmth coating my cheek. I jump and struggle against the chair, desperate to get away.

His head rolls to the side and his bloody hand drops. His face is so close, I'm forced to watch as he fades. I squeeze my eyes shut and turn my face against the floor to hide.

The door crashes open and Rachel screams again.

"Gabby, oh my God, we found you."

"Dustin?" I can't believe he's here.

"We're here. You're safe." He crouches beside me, touches the blood on my face. "Are you hurt?"

"No. That's his blood."

Dustin crouches and checks Herbert for signs of life.

"He's dead," I whisper.

Lucas fills the room next.

"You got him," Dustin congratulates Lucas.

Relief floods me at the sight of Lucas' broad body.

"Take care of Gabby, I'll help Rachel," Dustin says, taking control.

Lucas kneels and cuts the tape holding me to the chair. As soon as I can move, I crawl across the floor to his embrace. I don't question how he got here, just melt into his chest. He holds me tight, nearly crushing me to him. The safety of his arms breaks me and I give into the fear and shock. Heavy sobs of relief and sorrow.

"Shh. I've got you. You're safe now." His voice in my ear is beautiful music.

"I knew you would come," I whisper. "I was stalling him, waiting for you."

His arms tremble around me, his chest heaves and he fights back his own tears. His hands run over my hair, down my back. I push farther against him like a frightened child.

I breathe.

"Oh my God, Gabby!" Preston's voice breaks the sweet spell.

Lucas drops his arms and turns me over to Preston's embrace.

I allow Preston to hold me, but feel empty without Lucas's strength surrounding me.

"Why are you here?" I ask.

"He wouldn't stay home," Dustin says.

Preston helps me to my feet, hurries me out of the room away from the dead man on the floor.

I fight the urge to look over my shoulder at Lucas, but follow Preston outside.

Sirens sing in the distance and soon red and blue lights up the sky.

Preston tries to console me as we wait for the ambulance and police to arrive. He wants to hold me, to comfort me.

I don't want to be touched.

I'm uncomfortable with my left hand bare, and use my right glove to cover it. It fits awkwardly, but offers some security. I never want to touch anything again. I shove my hands in my pockets and sit on the front step.

Preston hovers close, pacing in his agitation.

"Preston, please sit down. You're making me nervous."

He joins me on the step, too close. I shift away putting a breath of distance between us.

"Thank you for helping find me," I manage to say.

Preston shrugs. "We were all scared for you, and for Rachel."

The ambulance pulls down the lane, saving me from further conversation.

A blur of officers and EMTs descend on the hidden trailer. I get checked out, but decline going to the hospital. I'm not hurt, physically. Psychically, I'm drained to the core.

They manage to release Rachel from her chains, and remove her on a stretcher. I hurry to her side, needing to see for myself she's okay.

"You were amazing," she whispers. "You were so brave, and I was so scared."

"We were both brave," I console.

"He killed them for me. All of them."

"He killed them for himself, for his own reasons. I saw it when I touched him. You are not to blame."

"Thank you," she whispers once more, and they load her into the ambulance.

Dustin and Lucas direct the rest of the team. With nowhere else to go, I sit in the grass with Preston by my side. He doesn't try to hold me, or ask me questions. I'm thankful for his quiet presence.

Lucas eventually comes to find me.

"You doing okay?"

I force a tired smile. "I guess. When can I go?"

"You'll have to give a formal statement, but we can wait until tomorrow. Sure you don't need a hospital?"

"I just need a bed. I could sleep for days."

Lucas's shoulders shift, uncomfortable.

"You want to ask me something. Just ask."

"What was he making you do in there?"

"He forced me to touch mementos from other murders, see the killings. He wanted me to prove I wasn't a fake."

Lucas and Preston make sounds of disgust.

"There are other victims," I say quietly. "I saw two of them, but he had more things in the drawer."

I shudder. I know what he wants to ask me, so I save him forming the words.

"I can touch them and tell you who they are. Not now," I add quickly. "Later, when I'm rested. Those women deserve justice."

Lucas starts to reply but doesn't get the chance

"Gabriella, oh my!" Grandma Dot's voice carries over the scene and her small but powerful frame pushes past the police tape. An officer tries to stop her, but her withering look makes him back away.

"It's okay, let her pass," Lucas says to the officer. "You won't stop her anyway."

I welcome Grandma Dot's touch, let her fawn over me, checking me for injuries the EMTs might have missed. It reminds me when I fell off my bike at her house when I was young. The memory warms.

"Is this blood? Did he cut you?"

"It's not my blood," I explain.

Grandma turns to Lucas. "I'm taking her home. She needs tea and a shower and a bed. You can worry about all your police stuff later."

Lucas can't hide a smile.

"Grandma Dot, what are you doing here?" Dustin interrupts. "This is a crime scene, not a family reunion."

"I'm taking Gabriella home."

"Can you take Preston home, too?" I ask. Grandma finally notices Preston at the edge of our group.

"Of course." She looks at Dustin in challenge.

"Fine. Take them both. I will need statements tomorrow."

Grandma Dot wraps her arm around my shoulders and steers me towards the road. Preston follows dutifully.

"Wait," I say and hurry back to Dustin.

"Um, there's something in my pocket I need to return," I say to my brother.

"What is it?"

"A piece of finger bone from Karen Jennings."

His eyes flash with confusion and anger.

"I didn't mean to take it. I accidentally held on to it that first day at the dig site. It needs to be returned to her."

"You're always full of surprises." He takes a plastic bag from his pocket and snaps it open.

"Can you get it? I don't want to touch it again."

His expression softens and he retrieves the bone.

"Get some rest. I'm sure Grandma's tea will help," he says gently, brotherly.

"I will."

He moves like he wants to hug me, but changes his mind and pats me on the shoulder instead. I don't mind. The simple act of affection warms me.

He turns on his heel, and goes back to work.

The three of us ride in silence in Grandma Dot's flatbed. The rhythm of the truck lulls me to sleep and I doze on the drive.

Parked in Preston's driveway, I bolt awake, confused and scared.

"Shh," Grandma Dot soothes and pats my knee. "We're just dropping him off."

I turn blurry eyes to Preston. "Thank you for your help." The words feel inadequate.

"Can we talk tomorrow?" he asks hopefully.

"Sure. But not before noon." I try to make a small joke.

He looks longingly at me and climbs out.

"He's nice," Grandma Dot says.

"Yes he is." I lean against her shoulder and doze again.

Grandma's tea, a hot shower and my childhood bed wrap me in comfort. Grandma sits on the edge of the bed with Jet on her lap, tucking me in like a child.

I get the courage to say what's bothering me.

"I didn't know it was him. I saw him every day at work and never sensed he was evil."

"There's no way you could have known." She brushes my damp hair off my face, careful not to touch my scar.

"But I should have. I could have saved Rachel before she was kidnapped. Maybe I could have saved those other women too."

"Gabriella, listen to me." Grandma turns my chin, forcing me to meet her eyes. "That man made the choice to hurt others. It's not your responsibility, it's his. This gift will bring you into contact with things you can't control. You have to do as much good as you can with it, but you aren't responsible for what others do."

She lets go of my chin and I curl deeper into the pillow. "I should have known," I mumble.

Nothing she can say will change how I feel, so she lets me sleep.


The next few days are a blur of questions. And answers.

I follow through on my promise to give names to Herbert's other victims. Six women were tortured by him in addition to Karen and Steven. With each item, I struggled not to see how their lives ended, just get their names.

I saw their deaths anyway.

Their stories are part of me now.

Lucas handled letting me touch the items. Dustin wasn't there. I'm fine with that. Our fragile re-bonding might crumble if he actually watches me do what I do. Lucas kept his reactions professional, but the glitter of awe in his eyes was evident. His acceptance gave me the courage to do them all. Six families were granted closure.

Lacey Aniston did a story about Herbert and what

happened in his trailer. I braced myself for the worst when I watched the coverage. To her credit, she didn't make any direct derogatory comments about me and my involvement. I didn't want to throw something at the TV when I watched it. It was the best I could expect from Lacey.

The highlight for me was meeting with Seth and Nicholas and Patrick. We meet in the day room at Life Village. Patrick seems lighter, more focused on the present. Seth gushes his appreciation, and I do my best to accept it graciously.

"I'm not sure what I did. Mostly I got kidnapped, and Lucas and Dustin actually stopped him," I point out.

"You risked your life to save our dad," Seth tries.

I don't correct him.

Even Nicholas concedes I helped them. He wears a polo and khakis, not his suit and tie. I like him better in his dressed-down clothes. He even shakes my hand. I wear gloves of course, but I'm surprised he'd even touch me.

I kneel in front of Patrick's wheelchair, join him on his level so I can see directly into his eyes. "You can put Karen to rest now," I say simply.

The fragile man touches my cheek, the same cheek Herbert smeared his blood on.

"Bless you." The two words are enough.

The intimacy of the meeting presses uncomfortably, and I make my exit as politely as I can.

"Will you come to Mom's funeral?" Seth asks. "It will be small, just family and close friends."

266

I hesitate. I didn't know Karen in life, but feel close to her in her death.

"I'll be there."

I attend the funeral alone. I toyed with the idea of bringing Preston, but decided against it. Our budding romance has been on hold the last few days. Preston has given me my space. He checks on me, is friendly, but he doesn't press. I appreciate the space more than I can explain.

Patrick Jennings sits in the front row, flanked by his sons. He seems stronger than when I saw him in the nursing facility just a few days ago. Seth told me he was improving every day, might even get to go back to his apartment soon. I'm proud of the part I played in his recovery.

The casket is small, only holding the bones of the woman. At the end of the service, everyone lines up to pay their last respects at the coffin before they lower it into the grave. Many people touch the casket lid as a show of respect.

Even with my thickest wool gloves on, I don't touch it.

I stand to the side, waiting to talk to Seth and his family. My neck tingles as if someone watches me. I look over my shoulder on reflex.

Far in the distance, a man turns and walks away.

Even through the yards and years separating us, I recognize the shape of the man, the way he walks.

"Dad?"

## THE END

**A note from the author:**

I truly hope you enjoyed this first book in Gabby's adventures. I certainly enjoyed writing it. Countless times Gabby surprised even me with her courage and her quirkiness. I am excited about telling the rest of her stories to you.

Reviews are very important to authors. If you enjoyed this book, or even if you didn't, please take a moment to leave a review on Amazon and let me know.

Be the first to know about new releases and what I am up to by joining my newsletter. By signing up you can read a **FREE** short story I wrote in high school (1990). **"My Name is Mud"** won the Grand Prize in the Northeast Indiana Young Writers Contest at the time. Sign up at DawnMerriman.com.

You can also join my fan club on Facebook I post fun stuff, book excerpts, hold contests and have fun with my fans.

People often ask me how I get ideas for my writing. I can't explain where they come from, only that it's from a power greater than myself and I feel truly blessed to tell my character's stories. I do listen to a lot of music to keep up the energy and tap into my creativity. It's a running joke at my house that if Mom has her headphones on you're going to hear some loud and bad singing.

Some characters even have their own theme songs to help me get into their heads. The following are songs that played a large part in getting me through Gabby's story. Please check them out and support these artists.

Gabby's theme Song: *"Bloodstream"* by Ed Sheeran
Lucas' theme Song*: "Making Love out of Nothing at All"* by Air Supply
Karen and her family's theme song: *"Photograph"* by Ed Sheeran
Killer's theme songs: *"Bandito"* by Twenty One Pilots and *"I Don't Care Anymore"* by HELLYEAH.
Other important songs I basically play on repeat as I work:
*"Neon Gravestones"* by Twenty One Pilots
*"Heathens"* by Twenty One Pilots
*"Getting Away With It"* by James
*"The Girl You Think I Am"* by Carrie Underwood
*"Waiting for the Miracle"* by Leonard Cohen
*"You Want it Darker"* by Leonard Cohen
Thank you for your interest in my work! Without readers, writers are just people typing alone. Each and every one of you are important to me, and I hope my stories touch you in some way.

God Bless,

**Dawn Merriman**